SHIT JUST GOT 2 REAL

TRIPLE J'S STORY PART 2

THE EXECUTIVE HOMEBOY

CONTENTS

AUTHOR PAGE

The Executive Homeboy is an award winning, Urban Novel Author with the natural gift of creative writing. He's the Chief Executive Officer of the Atlanta based investment company, Farm Houze Group LLC. For more information on the Author **visit: www.theexecutivehomeboy.com**

SYNOPSIS

Falling down a flight of stairs, inside the Fulton Jail, James "Triple J" Johnson, Jr finds himself waking in Atlanta's Memorial Hospital, Intensive Care Unit. With stress piled on top of stress, the news of the State seeking the death penalty in his case was enough to hospitalize any man that cares to live.

Struggling with his post-coma crippling, Triple J pushes himself to a speedy recovery, after rumor spreads of him possibly being a government informant. With repetitive jail-house workouts and physical therapy shockwave treatment, Triple J recovers a whole lot sooner than doctors predicted.

When his wife and right-hand man turn their backs on him, his father notifies him of his stage four kidney cancer and on top of all that a 28 member ANW Rico Indictment, Triple J is forced to make immediate adjustments within the organization, so that the spirit of the Ape continues to live for the generations to come.

Shit Just Got 2 Real.

PROLOGUE

$\mathscr{F}$rozen between the veil of life and death, James "Triple J" Johnson, Jr. lies immobilized as he struggles to explore the foreign area in which he is in. He blinks his eyes several times, in an effort to focus his vision, but is still only able to see the three feet blur ahead of him.

"My Baby! My Baby!" he hears the cries of a hysterical woman calling from above.

He attempts to turn in the direction of the call, but his frozen soul only stiffens.

Deep down in the dark shadows, several foreign figures race in the direction of the sitting soul, seeking to take possession. As they're reaching for the unaware Triple J, he's quickly snatched away and protected by a group of male warriors.

Shirtless in African tribal dress, they surround Triple J and provide an elite level of protection for him, carrying the crime boss to the shore line. With razor sharp, pointed edge spears, aimed and ready, they move in unison. Ready to take on the grim creatures. Knowing there was a certain defeat, against the battle-ready warriors, the grim creatures lash out in a temper fit. Their aggressive outpouring of anger creates large water waves for the warriors to fight back to the shore line. Despite the light water struggle, they keep aim with their weapons, forcing the grim creatures to stay back.

"My Baby!" the woman screams again, as she fights against an entourage of village women, holding her at the water's edge. "Ase! Ase! Ase!" She begins to chant with the rest of the village women.

Triple J's carried into a large straw structure, where he's taken before several members of his ancestral authority. Before he's placed before them the eldest male father calls for him.

"Bring him to me," he says in an authoritarian voice.

Dressed in royal purple and gold dashiki clothing, with a tall golden staff in hand, Baba Benji walks over to a table covered with burning candles. He grabs a gold flask and takes a quick sip of the strong warming liquid.

The rescuing warriors approach Baba Benji, carrying Triple J's frozen body, and at three feet away he quickly spins about face spraying his grandson with the burning liquid from his mouth.

Triple J immediately regains his mobility, standing on his own. Loud cheers erupt, echoing throughout the village and several men begin to beat Djembe Drums, signaling that he's alive.

The crying woman rushes inside, doing a spiritual dance with her arms as she runs towards Triple J. She grabs a hold of Triple J's by the neck pulling him to the ground as she falls.

"My Baby!" she sings as she's holding the face of her only child.

Face to face with his biological mother, Triple J stares at her and tears begin to form in his eyes. His mother transitioned when he was only three years old, leaving the young James with a yearning for a mothers love. He lays his head on her shoulder as they hug, grasping to her tightly.

For several seconds, they embraced one another and Baba Benji returned to his seat. He gives the two of them time together before interrupting their reunion.

"Hem, eem," Baba says as he clears his throat, "My child, I know this time with our James brings joy to your heart, but right now I'm sorry we don't have much time. He has to get back." Baba Benji says as he stares at them along with the rest of the ancestral order.

"My son, it's great to have you here with us but your time has yet to come. For all of your life this ancestral panel has witnessed you do well for yourself, reaching levels of success that very few in this family have reached. Speaking on behalf of this ancestral panel of four fathers I must admit we are astounded with your level of success.

Recently, you called upon the heavens, seeking to learn your purpose. Throughout your life, you've been an outstanding leader, guiding many in the direction in which you saw fit. You've been an ambassador to black imperialism but now is the time we exchange those wicked ways for wonderful wonders.

The days to come before you are going to be rougher than anything you've ever experienced, but in the end, everything is going to work out for your good." Baba Benji says before smashing his staff three times into the floor.

A smile stretches across Triple J's mother's face and tears begin to flow from her eyes. Triple J's escorted away by the rescue warriors and as he is leaving music is played as everyone bids him farewells.

"I Love You," his mother says while waving goodbye.

As he's being escorted away, the words of his grandfather replays in his head, *"The days to come before you are going to be rougher than you've ever experienced, but in the end, everything is going to work out for your good."*

As things get dark Triple J's life begins to play before him. All is well, until he sees himself standing in a crowded courtroom.

"We the jury find defendant James Johnson, Jr…,"

Shit Just Got 2 Real.

1

$\mathcal{S}$everal beeping indicators are heard by the comatose crime boss, as he slowly regains his consciousness. Struggling to open his eyes, Triple J battles against the dried film that's built up over his eyes. He attempts to wipe at it with his right hand, but the involuntarily, worn hand restraints limit his movement to the bed railing.

Over the last four months, a medically induced coma has consumed his life. After suffering a severe head injury, due to violently falling down a full flight of stairs inside the Fulton Jail, doctors initially gave the crime boss a slim chance of recovering. With severe brain swelling and little to no brain activity at times, discussions were being conducted on if the life support plug should be pulled on the crime boss.

Neither member of Triple J's team of doctors honestly believed he would ever wake up. Based on their records, most of them had the crime boss written off.

While conducting their final test before the decision was made, Triple J vitals were activated.

"Wow! This is a miracle," one of the doctors says while looking at his brain's CT scan results.

The CT scan results showed high volumes of brain activity and the medical staff were forced to let him live.

"Aaah," the crime boss groans as he slowly wakes up.

The low cries wake the sleeping Deputy James and she immediately leans up in her chair. Over the last three months she'd been at Triple J's bedside. Today was the first time she'd ever heard him groan like this. Adrenaline races through her veins, forcing her to jump to her feet, and race to the hospital's room door.

"Nurse! Nurse! Nurse!" She yells down the never-ending hallway, "He's waking up."

As if she was angered, a slim black nurse in solid dark purple scrubs peeps around the hall from the nurse's station with her hand on hip. Infectious excitement hit her finally understanding, she too became extremely hype, rushing from her desk to the crime boss's room.

"It's Johnson's room!" she relayed to the other nurses.

A group of four followed behind her, all racing towards Triple J's room. Deputy James waved her head rapidly, signaling for them to hurry as his groans grew louder.

Over the hospital's intercom, a 'Code Orange' was called.

"He's awake! He's awake!" Deputy James repeated excitedly.

This kind of excitement was unusual to have for an inmate, one of the nurses thought.

Little did she know Triple J and Deputy James had history.

When Triple J was first booked into the Fulton Jail, Deputy James was just an intake officer. They met while she was escorting him to the 6th floor, where the city's most violent inmates were housed. Before realizing he was the ANW Crime Boss, she thought he too was Just Another Inmate Lying (JAIL). Triple J surprised her using his gift of gab and won over her heart.

As the medical staff flooded the room Deputy James watched from the corner.

"We need these removed," Nurse Pam the charge nurse says, referring to the handcuff on Triple J's left hand.

Moving rapidly through the small crowd, Deputy James uses her 3-inch handheld handcuff key and removes them from him and the bed.

"Hey Mr. Johnson, this is Nurse Pam. Can you hear me?" She asks while grabbing Triple J's hand.

A second nurse wipes his face with a wet wipe, softening the crust around his eye before watching his eyelids fling open with life.

Triple squeezes her hand twice signaling, *Thank you.*

The hand squeezing response, signaled to the veteran nurse that he was alert and his chances of recovering were very high.

Flooding into the hospital room a team of white coats step in and take over.

"How's the patient's vitals?" One of them asked.

"Blood pressure 120/80. Pulse and temp are normal sir," Nurse Pam says.

"Wonderful," he responded.

Before Triple J's vitals were very low and his chances of recovering were slim to none.

Staring around the room like a baby fresh out the wound, Triple J cringes as they surround him.

"Hey Mr. Johnson, I'm Doctor Frank Cook. Do you know where you are right now?" Dr. Cook ask's standing at his bedside.

Triple J tried to speak but struggles from dry mouth.

"Let's get him some water," Doctor Cook said, recognizing his inability to speak.

Nurse Pam quickly grabbed his hospital thermal, the one she refilled every morning she worked, and placed the plastic straw in his mouth. Thankful for the cool liquid running down his throat he looked up in the air. Scanning the room, he got a glimpse of the white board behind her. Startled immediately, he looks around the room for the phone in a slight panic but doesn't see one.

Dr. Cook sees that he's very alert and calms him as he continues his questioning.

"Hey! Hey! Mr. Johnson calm down," after seeing a spike in Triple J's heart rate. "Do you know where you are," he asks for a second time.

"Yes! A damn hospital," he responds in anger.

"It's okay Mr. Johnson. Do you know how you got here?"

Triple J begins to explore his brain searching for what could have caused him to be in the hospital.

I remember Officer Williams that "The Super Cop MFer", kicking in my door, finding the stash me and Ape Shit Flamez had. Then Lt. Rodgers, fine ass, giving me some of that good pussy before my wife, Jessica, heard the two of us bragging about our sexual explosion. I remember her being pissed and real emotional but I thought it was just from me being locked up. There's a fetus growing in her wound and I'm about to be a dad," Triple J thought to himself.

Still thinking about Dr. Cook's questions, Triple J continued scanning his brain.

I remember that airplane stewardess, sending that letter claiming to also be pregnant, right before my lawyer dropped a huge bomb shell on me. The State was trying to give me the death penalty. I remember–chest pains striking me and I stopped at the stairs.

It was like a light bulb clicked in his head, the way his face lit up before his response.

"I must've fell down the stairs," Triple J answers Dr. Cook.

"Yes! You actually fell down those stairs pretty hard," Dr. Cook responded. Shocked to see that he remembered. "Do you know what today's date is?" He continued.

"Yes, it's my wife's birthday," Triple J responded, shocking the whole room.

"And what day is that?" Dr. Cook asked.

"February 21st" Triple J answered and the whole room erupted in applause.

Triple J didn't understand why everyone was so happy. All of the nurses and medical staff expected him to be out of his mind, but he was well aware. Deputy James stared at him with her hands pressed to her in prayer as tears of joy ran down her face.

"He's back y'all" Dr. Cook said excitedly over the crowd of cheers. "Welcome back Mr. Johnson," he said while shaking Triple J's hand.

After everyone in the room calmed, Dr. Cook went over the series of events that took place while Triple J was in the coma.

"You've been in a coma for over four months now Mr. Johnson," he begins to say. "In Med school, our professors always told us about Miracle patients. 'You'll have at minimum one Miracle Patient in your career they would say. I've been a MD 14 years now and today you've become my first, Miracle Patient. I just wanna shake your hand again and tell you Thank You." Dr. Cook continued before they all left.

Deputy James closed the door to their room before she returned to Triple J's bedside.

"Hey, how you feeling, King," she asked him in a low tone. Triple J cut his eyes at her like he was annoyed. "Don't do that, James," she replied sadly.

"Don't do what? Pull a you on you. You could have came to see me at any time but decided not to," Triple J says angrily.

"It wasn't me," Deputy James says.

"The first step to recovery is admitting that you have a problem. You over here with this cry baby shit like you didn't abandon me. What am I supposed to do forgive you?" Triple J asks her.

"It wasn't me!" Deputy James yells. "My uncle is the Captain. You know the crazy old man, Captain James! He caught me coming out of your dorm on the night I last saw you, Bae. He told me I had to stay away from you. It was something big about to go down and I didn't need to be involved."

"What do you mean something big?" Triple J asked.

"I don't know, Bae. All I know is when I came to work the next day, I couldn't come inside the jail. I had been transferred here, to hospital duty."

Deputy James saw that he was deep and thought and wanted to make things right with him. Triple J was indeed her jailhouse Bae. The entire time he'd been in the coma she'd been at his bedside. Although he was unresponsive, she talked with him, prayed for him and even read him books aloud.

Her favorite was *Love Always* By Deshion Hightower.

If only he knows how much I cared for him, she thought.

"What can I do to make our life better, Bae?" She asked.

At the time, Triple J couldn't think about anything other than today was his wife's birthday.

"I need to use the phone," he says after a brief pause.

Reaching behind his bed she grabs the hospital's phone.

"Technically, I can lose my job for letting you use the phone. To be honest I don't care because I'll do anything for you King," she says with a smile on her face.

He grabs hold of the phone when she passes it to him. He's forced to take a brief pause as he searches his brain for his wife's number. Nearly half a minute passes as it suddenly becomes clear and his fingers start dialing.

Several rings go by before she answers.

"Hold on! It's the hospital," Jessica says between giggles.

"Fuck them folks. All they can say now is if the nigga dead or not," Triple J hears a familiar male voice say before the two are heard kissing.

"Hold on!" Jessica says again in between giggles, "Hello, I already gave y'all permission to do what you have to do," she continues.

In two point five seconds, their entire relationship flashes through his mind. Tears begin to slowly flow from his eyes as the betrayal settles in his heart.

"Hello?" Jessica says screaming into the phone, "Can y'all hear me?"

"Yes I'm here!" Triple J replies with a voice filled with sadness. "Just called to say Happy Birthday,ontinued before ending the call.

Shocked, surprised and extremely hurt Triple J tries to process it all as he squeezes the phone.

Hearing his right hand man, JT Wolf, voice in the background kissing with his wife was the biggest betrayal known to man.

Shit Just Got Real before but now *Shit Just Got 2 Real*..

2

a s tears pour from the crime bosses' eyes, he presses his head deep into the medical pillow. His wife's infidelity on top of his medical trauma left Triple J in emotional turmoil. As the thoughts race through his mind about what has taken place with his two most trusted individuals. *All I've done for these motherfuckers, this how they repay me,* Triple J thinks to himself. *I've cheated on my wife in the past but I would have never smashed her cousin, her closest relative. On her birthday! Really?* He continues.

Oblivious to what's taken place on the call, Deputy James wonders what's happened for Triple J to have the vicious rage fill his eyes all of a sudden. Attempting to console him she massages her phone from his tight grip.

"Bae, it's gone be okay. I'm here with you," she says in a soft motherly melodic voice.

Triple J looks into her eyes and sees the genuine feelings she has for him.

Her eyes are beautiful, he thinks. *They're just not the eyes I want looking at me right now.*

Triple J begins to think about all the times he's cheated on his wife and the pain he put her through.

"I guess this is payback from way back," he tells Deputy James.

Still oblivious to what he's saying, she just nods her head in agreement.

Since leaving the jail, Deputy James has yearned for the crime boss by the second. Every day as she watched over him, she craved her some Triple J. Her urge to see his cock size was so high but she declared to wait until he woke from his coma before she looked. When doctors began conversing about pulling the plug, she refused to accept that because she knew her time with him was sure to come.

Upset with his wife, the timing was perfect for the craving deputy. Taking advantage of the situation, Deputy James continued to console him, sliding her hand underneath his bed sheet. Fondling with his manhood, she gets him to power up the long way. Triple J closes his eyes and lays his head back into the pillow as she jerks her hands up and down the thick girth of his rod.

The touch of a woman is much needed right now, Triple J thinks.

Unsatisfied with just touching, Deputy James lowers the bed rail on the right side of the bed. All this time she's waited now was her time to have him inside of her mouth. Grabbing the pillow from the sofa chair she'd been sitting in next to him all this time, she lays it on the floor next to him. Pulling back the bed sheet, she lowers her head into his lap as she falls to her knees. Giving him a warm welcome into her mouth she introduces Triple J to another side of her love.

"Eeek," he screams in sexual satisfaction.

Deputy James mouth was a water fountain and she flooded the crime boss as she sucked and slurped his mans.

She trying to suck the soul out of my body, Triple J thinks.

Loving how he tastes, Deputy James continues to please him. Refusing to take a breathing break she continues to go hard until he ejaculates inside of her mouth.

Laying in despair with his mouth wide open, Triple J was unable to make a sound. Possessed by the pleasure that he felt, Triple J fell victim under the love spell of the deputy. Deputy James had taken complete control of every organism in his body massaging the magic muscle in his body.

As the emission pressure built up, Triple J's heart rate and blood pressure spike, sending an alert to the nurse's station. Deputy James continues to suck him off, oblivious to the alarm that's going off. She goes extra hard as his rod expands more inside of her mouth. Triple J's whole body locks up and Deputy James lifts her head and pumps his penis so that his ejaculation can cover her face. Cum squirts heavily all over her face, sealing her right eye. Four months' worth of buildup.

Nurse Pam knocks at the door and quickly enters the hospital room, checking on Triple J's health status. Her immediate reaction was total surprise. This was enough to drive a preacher wild wild west. Deputy James turns towards her with semen spread all over her face.

Nurse Pam looks and sees that the bed rail is down and Triple J's bed sheets are pulled back. High on euphoria she sees him lying at full erection, with a photographic smile covering his face. Infected by their energy, Nurse Pam also puts on a huge smile as she stares back and forth at the two of them.

"Y'all set the alarm off," she says walking over to the blue monitor.

After clicking several buttons on the screen, she looks back over at Triple J and his erect penis, "I'm glad you're doing okay in that department," she continues. As she's leaving the room, she looks back at the two of them and chuckles.

Shaking her head as she leaves out the door she says, "This Shit Just Got 2 Real."

3

*S*exually relieved, Triple J laughs at the thoughts of Jessica and JT messing around. *They think they're playing me, but I'm gone show them why I'm Triple J the King of the Apes,"* he says to himself.

Triple J looks over at Deputy James as she's cleaning her face. *Damn shawty you really fuck with me,* he says to himself. *You ain't give a damn about getting cum all over ya face.* He continues to think. Triple J continues to watch her as she cleans her face, wiping the side of her mouth.

There was something he felt with Deputy James, but it was nothing like the feelings he had for his wife. James and Jessica once had a bond so tight that twins joined at the hips would have gotten jealous at how close they were. Sexually relieved when Triple J squirted out onto the Deputy face, he let go of everything that he and Jessica ever had, business and all.

She can have that shit, he says to himself. *One thing about it if she fucking with that lame ass nigga, she gone lose it all in a matter of time.*

Remembering what his father taught him about putting all your eggs in one basket, Triple J made sure to put some funds away. It was, one million exactly he had stashed in an offshore account, specifically for "lord have mercy" times like this.

Laying in one spot on the hospital bed, Triple J struggles to turn over into a better position.

"You need some help?" Deputy James asks him while approaching his bed side.

"Yes! Please," He responds truthfully.

Remembering her training, she lifts his right leg towards his chest, bending it into a 90-degree angle at the knee. Next, she pushes his knee towards the opposite side of his body, positioning his body to be lifted. Sliding her hand under his arm she lifts his body helping him to stand.

"Damn you strong," Triple J says as she's lifting him. "You must be a powerlifter how easy you moved me." He continues sarcastically.

"I feel like that sometimes. Being a mother of three bad ass boys, working full time and on the side, I might as well be a powerlifter with all this weight I gotta carry," she says, raising her right arm into a flex.

Triple J hears the pain in her voice and immediately feels sympathetic for the young black queen. Sometimes you can see a person and think they got it all together but she was really dealing with a lot. He now understood why the captain wanted her to stay away from him. She was a young woman struggling to make things better for her youngins.

He looks Deputy James up and down, before spitting game at her..

"Three boys? I would have never guessed you had one," he says.

"Pisss! Boy Stop you know you lying. My ass use to be dumb fat before I had the twins."

"Twins?" Triple J asks.

"Yeah, I have 4 year old twin boys," she replies.

That was a turn on for him because he always wanted twins and knowing that she's carried them before was a wonderful situation, he thought.

"I still can't see you pushing out three big head lil boys. Two at the same time. You had to be good and doped up." He says.

"No, I had natural births in the swimming pool at home."

"In the swimming pool?" He says aloud.

"Not the kind of swimming pool you're thinking about," Deputy James laughs at him. "It's a blow up pool filled with water for when you have a natural birth."

Triple J had never heard of such a thing. As his memory slowly came back to him, he remembered the two women he had pregnant.

It's possible neither one of these babies can be mine, he thinks now that he's found out about Jessica and JT.

Triple J shakes his head as he begins to get upset again. *I let that shit go,* he says to himself.

"Do you wanna watch some TV?" Deputy James asks him as she grabs the remote control on the side of his bed.

"Yeah, that's cool," he replies nonchalantly.

As soon as she flips on the TV monitor a red Breaking News alert flashes across the screen.

Breaking News

"Happening right now, Doctors at Atlanta's Memorial Hospital are ready to give an update on the condition of Atlanta's most notorious crime boss James Johnson Jr. We have our lead reporter

Malissa Waters on the scene, Hey, Malissa. Are you there?" The studio anchor asks.

"Yes, John. I'm here outside of Atlanta's Memorial Hospital where it's being reported that Mr. James Triple J Johnson has in fact awakened after a four months comatose state. Doctors have reported he is in fact speaking and responding well to their test and verbal questions and looks to make a full recovery. This is good news because several months ago we reported on Mr.Johnson's murder indictment. The state made their intentions clear, that they were going to seek the death penalty on him. After his accident, their fear was that Mr. Johnson wouldn't be competent enough to stand trial, if and when he recovered from his coma. My sources at the DA's office have reported to me that they in fact still have every obligation in protecting the community from crime polluting individuals like Mr. Johnson and wish to punish him by death."

Triple J looked over at Deputy James and they both stared at each other in disbelief. He knew in the life he was living; things would someday come to an end. But never could have guessed it would be publicly broadcasted like this.

Deputy James sees the heartbreak in his eyes and can tell he's really damaged. She stands up to turn off the TV, but before she does Triple J stops her. The camera man leaves his shot of Malissa Waters and scans the crowd of Triple J supporters gathered outside of the hospital. He sees them holding signs one reading "Get well Triple J."

"Do you think I would be able to see them from the window?" he asks.

"You should, I don't see why not," Deputy James says.

She lets down the bed rail on the side closest to the window before she helps him lean up. With his feet hanging off to the side of the bed he tries to stand, but his legs are like jello. He shakes violently before falling flat onto the floor.

Deputy James tries to catch him but the way he dropped you would have thought a taser was deployed. Triple J looks up at her in disbelief, totally surprised that he can't walk. He thought back for a second, *the doctors didn't say anything about me being paralyzed.* He actually wasn't but something that he did know was that if he couldn't walk, *Shit Just Got 2 Real.*

4

Several very important calls were made immediately after Triple J awakened from his Coma. Hospital doctors and administrators were in a custody battle with the Sheriff's office and other state agencies over the proper care providers for the crime boss. Because Triple J was actively in the Sheriff's custody, they were responsible for all medical care and expenses under the 8th Amendment. Triple J's already been in the ICU over the last four months and his medical expenses had grown extensively. Although he was currently awake and the test results were looking good, hospital doctors recommended he remain under their care for at least another week's time. The sheriff's office argued that Triple J being housed at a public hospital was a security threat being that he's a very powerful man. They knew that anytime with his political and criminal ties he could orchestrate an escape plan.

The hospital's staff and administrators argued that because he's been under their care for so long, they should keep him for at least another week to observe his progress.

Although Triple J appeared to be in good health, if not properly treated he could potentially start having complications that require immediate attention. If he's not on the hospital's monitors and his health takes a nosedive, the hospital holds liability because they refused to follow protocol.

All parties involved knew it really wasn't about Triple J's health. Their conflict was about the money. Who was going to pay who and for what?

After a quick and thorough hearing, it was clear that the jail had the most expenses. They were paying there deputies to sit with him and medical bills that continued to pile up as long as the crime boss to be there.

After long hours of debate a conclusion was made. Triple J would be transported back to the Fulton Jail and housed in the Medical Observation Unit. For the transfer several tactical trained deputies were called in, including SWAT. Ever since the news updated his status, several black males have been stopped from roaming unauthorized areas of the hospital. Police and hospital security were unable to associate them to Triple J or his ANW crew, but the Sheriff's office still took the precautions.

Outside the hospital, large crowds continued to gather as deputies grouped to transport the crime boss. Spotting the police's caravan on the side of the hospital, one of the protesters look out alert the others and they flood the area with protesters. Many of them held "Get Well," signs and balloons in support for the crime boss's recovery.

Ready to move, the entire side of the hospital where Triple J was located went on lockdown. No one was allowed to move except the Sheriff's staff and EMT that were a part of the transporting team.

"You gone be okay," Deputy James whispered to him as they began to roll his hospital bed out into the hallway.

Waiting outside of his room was a fleet of sheriff deputies and two paramedics. They had a stretcher prepared for him to roll on during transport. Sliding him across the bed onto the stretcher they did quickly by snatching the bed sheet.

As they began to roll, the tactical team surrounded his bed with machine guns ready across their chest.

"Damn, all this for me?" He asked dumbfounded but neither of them answered. "This Shit Just Got 2 Real" he continued.

One of the tactical dressed deputies spoke into his headset mic, in a number code Triple J was unable to translate.

"Floor 3 clear for 1027," he said before taking a brief pause, "copy, we're on the move."

They then proceeded rolling Triple J onto a medical elevator where his bed was pushed flush against the wall. The team of deputies filed in on side of him. Triple J looked around and saw that they all had murderous looks in the eyes like today's operation wasn't about transporting him but taking him out.

I wish they sent the Marshals, at least those guys were gentlemen, he thought, reminiscing about his flight back to Atlanta.

When the elevator doors opened Triple J saw that they were exiting on the B level, which usually represented the bottom or basement. A second group of tactical dressed officers were there waiting on him with another patient.

Since I been gone, they must have declared Martial Law or something, he thought as he was being exchanged with another patient. Down a long tunnel the paramedics preceded until they reached the lower level of the children's hospital.

When Triple J saw the signs, he slowly began to realize then what was taking place. *The children's hospital sits across the street from the main hospital. So, they must be sneaking me out the back,* he thought.

They moved rapidly through the lower level, almost as if someone was chasing them. Quickly reaching a second elevator with the doors ready for them to enter, they rolled Triple J in and the group also filed in on side of him. He was taken to the dock level, where several trucks and vans were waiting for them outside.

The paramedics rolled Triple J out to their truck where he was rolled through the doors of the ambulance.

"Y'all did a great job," the lead member said to the team "I'll see you on the other side. Let's move out," he continued in an authoritarian voice.

One of the paramedics climbed in back with Triple J, along with one of the tactical deputies.

"How you feeling?" The EMT asked.

"I'm okay, just ready to get this over with," Triple J responded looking over at the deputy with the assault rifle dangling between his legs.

"I feel you," we should be there in no time. It's just down the road.

"Cool," Triple J responded.

Triple J sat back and closed his eyes thinking again about his wife and friend messing around.

I really don't get it. I could expect for him to backdoor me but not her agreeing to it. They sounded like a happy couple over the phone, like they been together for years. Have they been messing around behind my back all this time? Triple J questioned. *Or are they just getting cool since I been away?*

Triple J went deep into thought thinking of different times things seemed weird in their relationship.

Wow! They really working the move on me," he continued to think.

As he lays there he's quickly brought back to reality when he hears the safety of the deputy's weapon flip. Both Triple J and the paramedic look to the rear of the truck where he sits. With his hands ready on his weapon, he scans out the back window like he's looking for someone to approach. Both Triple J and the EMT sit in silence wondering what's taking place.

Over the constant medical monitors beeping, heavy radio chatter can be heard coming from the deputy's headset. As the truck begins to speed up, they begin to wonder what's really going on.

"Keep up with that van in front of you," the Deputy looks back and yells to the driver.

Triple J tries to fix himself on the bed after they make a quick and sharp turn.

"Don't move again, or I'll shoot you motherfucker," the Deputy yells at him.

Triple J's experience with law enforcement men hasn't been the best, especially with a super cop kind like this one. He knew they were already afraid of his reputation, Triple J sat stiff for the rest of the ride. Eyes locked in one place looking like a male manikin. Even when the truck went over the deadly Atlanta potholes he stayed as still as he could be. He knew police were getting away with killing black men all over the world right now, his best bet was to do whatever he said.

Bad mon wit da burner, Triple J thought how his childhood friend Senio would describe the police in his Jamaican accent.

For the rest of the ride, they drove at a high rate of speed, quickly getting to the Fulton Jail. Outside the truck several officers can be heard yelling and screaming at each other. As the deputy that rode with Triple J climbs out and joins the rest of his group their words can be heard clearly.

"Noo Holiday! Noo," you can hear one of them yell at the other.

"My fucking brother is dead because of this mother fucker and you wanna protect him."

Both Triple J and the EMT looked at each other in shock, realizing then that Shit Just Got 2 Real.

5

*W*heeled onto the third floor of Fulton Jail's medical observation unit, MOU; several members of the jail's medical staff and deputies can be seen surrounding a television. Stopping with Triple J in front of the glass booth, while they wait both the EMT's and Triple J locked in on the news also.

As they watched, Triple J began to realize that someone was trying to kill him according to the news headline.

Deputy deceased during an assassination attempt on local crime boss.

Now more attentive to the story Triple J began to wonder what had taken place.

Breaking News
"Yes David! We're outside of Atlanta's Memorial Hospital where our source from the Sheriff's office has confirmed that today one of their deputies was killed in the line of duty. As deputies were briefed today for a high-profile transport it's said they received

several tips, that members of the Apes & Wolves crime family were planning an escape for their leader Triple J. Triple J whose real name is James Johnson Jr. was indicted on a long length of charges several months ago one including murder. While awaiting trial inside of the Fulton Jail Triple J began having chest pains during a meeting with his well-known defense attorney Torris J Esquire. And those chest pains lead to him stumbling down a flight of stairs injuring his head severely. Those injuries put Mr. Johnson in a coma where he recently surprised doctors with his miracle awakening. During the transport deputies ran a double covert operation sneaking the crime boss out of the hospital through an undisclosed exit. While the second team carried out the public transport several masked gunmen ambushed the deputies flooding them with rapid rounds from high powered assault rifles. One deputy was pronounced dead minutes after being rushed back inside to ER, and two others were admitted with no life-threatening injuries. State investigators are on scene questioning witnesses and reviewing area surveillance for any tips on the masked men. If you have any information investigators ask that you call the Atlanta City's Police tips hotline number at 1866-Stop-Crime, again the number is 1833-Stop-Crime.

The split screen went back between both the anchor and news report. When the spectating staff turned their heads from the TV, Triple J turned his with them. He couldn't do much because he stood out like a sore thumb. Sitting in the middle of the floor strapped to a stretcher.

Everyone knew who he was and several faces stared at the crime boss from all sides of the room. A few of the nurses walked out of the booth and past the stretcher he laid in.

Sargent Carter, a veteran deputy exited the booth and his negative energy could be felt throughout the room. He approached the crime boss from the side of the stretcher and slammed a hard right hand into Triple J's right eye. Surprising both of the paramedics, one quickly grabbed the stretcher that began to tilt over while the other wrapped his arms around the Sargent that had his second hand ready to punch the crime boss again.

Several other members of the jail's security staff raced over to help the paramedics restrain the irate Sargent.

"This motherfucker is a dead man. He's a dead man," the Sargent repeated as he was being carried away.

Already physically disable, Triple J just stared at the Sargent and took a mental note.

You got to know you just fucked up big boy, he thought to himself.

The doors to the elevator behind them began to beep, and off came racing several ranking white shirts.

"What the hell is going on up here?" A voice yells that Triple J is very familiar with.

He looks to the side of his stretcher and sees the man who seems to always find him when something goes wrong, Captain James!

"Mr. Johnson!" He calls out with a surprised expression on his face. "Mann, it's been a minute how you feeling King," the Captain continues showing genuine concern.

"I need medical attention on my eye," Triple J answer's him as a stream of blood runs down his face from the corner of his eye.

One of the EMT's sees his wound and begins to pack it with surgical dressing. He places it over Triple J's cut eye cleaning the area before examining the wound.

"Is he going to need stitches?" Captain James asked the paramedic.

"Yes! This cut is nasty," the paramedic says as he begins to apply pressure to the fast-flowing cut.

"Okay, Let's take him to the clinic where the doctors are," Captain James tells the paramedics.

Leading them around the corner, Captain James takes them past a holding cell where several inmates begin to beat on the glass after seeing Triple J.

"There he goes," one of the younger guys says. "King Ape is back," he hears a different voice yell.

Yes, I'm back and things are about to go Ape Shit, Triple J thinks about his Baba's words.

The doctor immediately attends to Triple J instructing the nurse to check the crime bosses' vitals. She approaches him cautiously smiling while attending to the crime boss.

"How you feeling?" The young nurse asks him as he leans over on the stretcher.

Triple J makes eye contact with her and thinks about his current circumstances.

"Ion really know, how to feel right now," he answers in his native Atlanta slang.

"You gone be okay. Just keep God first in all that you do," she tells him.

After the vitals were taken, the doctor quickly patches him up, cleaning and sealing his cut with liquid stitches. Since the officer involved incident with Triple J, the entire jail has been on lockdown. Captain James rushes the doctor to clear him so they could get him to a cell. No inmates or staff members were allowed to move due to safety concerns.

As soon as the doctor cleared him, they started moving. In the hallway, Captain James had the paramedics switch Triple J from the hospital's stretcher to the jail's. With Captain James on the scene Triple J knew there was nothing for him to worry about now. The last he remembered he and the captain were in good standing but he could never put his guard down again. No one was to be trusted.

Around the corner he was taken to MOU. Captain James escorted Triple J and the paramedics to a medical cell built specifically for disable inmates.

Thinking the worst on his way to MOU, all he could think about was him having to lay on the small mattress again. Seeing the thick cushioned mattress in the medical cell, Triple J smiles.

This the real one, he says to himself thinking about the backbreaking bunk beds he was given when he first was arrested.

"I'll be right back to have a word with you Mr. Johnson," Captain James says as he closes the heavy metal door to his cell.

Damn, I'm locked in a cell again, Triple J says to himself as he looks around his new living quarters. For several long minutes he looks around the cell reflecting on what his life has become.

Robbed of his concentration he turns his gear around as the key is inserted into the sliding door.

He sees Captain James at the door, returning with his chain gang girlfriend, Lt. Rodgers.

"Heeyyy!" She sings in her melodic voice as she enters his cell first.

Triple J just smiles at the freaky deputy remembering the sexual times they had together.

"How are you feeling Mr. Johnson?" Lt. Rodgers asks while rubbing on his arms.

"Y'all gone have to get up at a later time," Captain James says to Lt. Rodgers interrupting her lovers reunion. "This is serious shit we need to talk about. As a matter of fact step out," he instructs the Lieutenant.

As soon as she closes the cell door, Captain James drops a bomb shell on the crime boss.

"So there's been a lot of discussions involving you lately Triple J and our staff have decided not to allow you back up on the floor," He says. "For your safety, we think it's best for you to stay down here even after you heel up."

"What's going on?" Triple asks as he struggles to sit up on the bed upset.

"Relax, Relax." Captain James says trying to calm the crime boss.

"Mr. Johnson?" The captain calls his name in a settled voice. "To be all the way honest with you, it's a lot going on within your organization. We know the truth but a jailhouse kite was intercepted by one of our staff members that included you. The word coming down from somebody at the top of ANW is that you're a rat. They're saying your jailhouse accident was a plot to get you out of the jail to spill inside information about your organization to law enforcement," Captain James says before Triple J interrupts him.

"A rat?" Triple J yells. "These niggas got me fucked up," he yells at the top of his lungs. "I ain't never told shit," Triple J continues.

Immediately Triple J gets upset, but he knew he had to calm down. The series of unknowing events started making sense since coming out of his coma. His ex-partner, JT Wolf, was laid up with his wife and they seemed like they were extremely happy together since he'd been out the way. The Sheriff's Deputies were ambushed at the hospital during the transfer and one died because they were going after the crime boss.

As things begin to clear up, Triple J realized that JT Wolf had declared war, this was about to crumble from the top.

First, they were wishing I died in the coma. Then put in the streets that I'm a rat. Tried to kill me at the hospital, and now the captain is telling me I'm going into involuntary protective custody.

"I need a burner phone?" Triple J tells the captain.

Captain James nods his head before stepping out of Triple J's cell.

Since they want war, okay I'll take em to war. Triple J says to himself.

Shit Just Got 2 Real.

6

Since receiving the news from Captain James, Triple J knew there wasn't too many he could trust. The rumors began roaming around the jail, stating that he was a police informant and that was not a good look.

In the underworld, everyone knew that the most difficult rumor to recover from was A Rat! Triple J knew there were moves that needed to be made for him to recover. He needed someone strong and bold, to carry things out for him.

The first person to come to his mind was his wife, as usual, but now she was the opposition. After a few seconds of deep thinking, he knew there was one friend he could call on, DonJuan Bennett.

DonJuan wasn't the closest associates Triple J had but they did manifest a lot of riches together. Triple J watched Mr. Bennett Pressure Washing LLC, business grow from a pickup truck, trailer and pressure washer to a fleet of commercial vehicles. They rolled out every morning tackling some of the toughest commercial and residential jobs throughout the Atlanta Metropolitan Area. Just after a few months in business, DonJuan gained contracts in all three branches of government. Mr. Bennett Pressure Washing had so much work coming in at one time that DonJuan had to call on his friend Triple J for a loan to supply the business when the banks wouldn't.

Triple J, always eager to help his friends, gave DonJuan the financial assistance with no interest on the back end.

"I owe you," DonJuan said at the time and he really meant that.

Little did he know now was the time to repay that favor.

Since coming out of the coma, Triple J began to notice he struggled to process thoughts that came to his mind. The last four digits of DonJuan's cell number just wouldn't come clear in his brain. The only number Triple J was able to remember clearly was the number to DonJuan's office.

Dialing in, Triple J made the call using the flip phone Captain James brought back to him. When the phone started ringing and a female voice answered, "Bennett Pressure Washing," Triple J was relieved because he knew that things would soon come together.

"Good Morning Ma'am. Is Mr. Bennet in today?" Triple J asked using his professional tone of voice.

"He is! Actually, he's in a meeting right now. May I take a message?"

"Yes please!" Triple J thought about how his government name was ringing all over the news. He knew he couldn't tell her his real name so he gave his moniker. "Tell him it's The Executive Homeboy with an urgent call," Triple J continues.

"Is it okay if I put you on hold for a second, The Executive Homeboy?" The receptionist asked.

"Yes! I'm here," He answers.

For a few minutes, Triple J waited for DonJuan to pick up on the call. As he waited, all he could think was, *DonJuan would be the perfect candidate for this job.*

Breathing heavy into the phone DonJuan picked up winded.

"Triple J! Hey Man what's going on? Are you out yet?" DonJuan asked, speeding with his words.

"Not yet big brother not yet," Triple J replied saddened. "And it's not looking good for me right now," he continued.

DonJuan could hear in his friend's voice that this call was because his friend was in a severe need of aid.

"You know this is my season," DonJuan began. "But a call from my most favorable friend comes like priority mail. You know what I mean? DonJuan asked.

"Yes, I do know," Triple J replied.

"Whatever you need Triple J I'm here just let me know," DonJuan continued offering assistance.

"I need you to go on a little vacation for me," Triple J says.

"Vacation? For how long?" he asked Triple J in a not so sure voice tone. "Because I swear to you, I'm in need of a long one," DonJuan continues with a smile.

Briefly, Triple J began to question himself thinking, *how did I pick the wrong man?* Until he realized that DonJuan was only teasing him.

Continuing, DonJuan asks, "Where exactly am I going?"

For sure he was the right man now, Triple J begins giving him instructions because shit was about to get too real.

"I need you to get a pen and write this down," Triple J says to him. "Let me know when you're ready," he continues.

"I'm ready," DonJuan answers with his pen ready on a yellow legal pad.

"You going to meet someone in Cuba," Triple J begins telling him.

"Okay! So how am I going to get into Cuba?" DonJuan asks knowing that traveling to the country was restricted coming from the United States.

But still he took notes knowing Triple J had a plan.

"You're going to meet with my pop and he's going to take you to one of my uncles that live in the country. When you meet him, he's going to give you a satellite phone. All you do is press 7 and the phone will begin dialing."

As DonJuan took notes he was surprised at how sophisticated things were already.

"You'll get instructions from the pilot and he's going to tell you where you need to meet him,"

"Okay," DonJuan replies as he's taking notes.

"Your first stop is going to be at a safety deposit box that I need you to access in Sweden. The key will be taped to the battery under the back cover of the yellow satellite phone. In that box is my deceased mother's gold pendant necklace. Put the necklace around your neck before you leave the vault. Make sure you wear the pendant under your shirt until you get to the private air strip in Cuba. There several henchmen will be waiting for you," Triple J pauses for a second. "When you land, show the necklace to the guys and they're going to escort you through the jungles. You're going to visit a weird looking old man and he's going to look at you very strangely when he sees the pendant around your neck. Bow your head to him and knock three times at his feet. When you stand back up, tell him you're there on my behalf and it's important that you see him now." Triple J closes out.

After giving DonJuan the instructions, forethought began

to take place. He knew the outcome of this situation was going to work in his favor.

Shit Just Got 2 Real.

7

$\mathcal{A}$tlanta's Fulton Jail was no playground and well known for its extreme violence. No matter where you were housed, if a situation sparked, things would go from peace to the place you wouldn't wanna be. Triple J knew that and was very much so aware of the environment. The smell of the jail constantly reminded him of the blood spilled all over the day room floor he saw his first day on the inside. Although he was physically handicap, mentally he was prepared to go hard anyway possible.

Inmate.com, the exclusive source of jail news, had multiple reports of midnight murders. The story was officers would sneak into the jail cells, during the late-night hours, killing inmates and make it appear to be a suicide. Crime scene investigators did very little to investigate since the staged scene looked so well set up.

Early the next morning, squeaky wheels could be heard rolling down the hallways. Triple J was awakened from his light sleep as he wondered what the strange noise could be.

Raising his head slightly he quickly realized it was only the chow train bringing breakfast.

Although he was cripple, Triple J knew he had to get up. Climbing out of bed was a struggle for him but it was something he had to do not to look weak.

You're either predator or prey, he reminds himself.

Getting in his chair was difficult and thoughts of giving up crossed his mind.

You should just wait for help; he says to himself but his heart wouldn't let him quit.

For several long minutes he struggled, until he finally made it. Winded and out of breath he remembered his martial arts training and began to breathe from his diaphragm. After catching his breath, he rolls his chair to the cell door, positioning his back towards the wall like he's still on the seventh floor, ready for whatever.

Damn, I'm fucked up, Triple J says to himself as he thinks about how incarceration has forced him to adjust in so many ways in so little time.

As he waited for the trays to come, he realized the medical floor was a little different than upstairs. Upstairs the officers picked guys that were assigned to the 7th floor to run around and assist them, medical was different. They used inmate workers.

Inmate workers are guys that are assigned to detail around the jail. They do the maintenance, sanitation, administration, clean up and medical. Unlike everyone else in the jail, they wear multicolor brown and blue scrubs with "inmate worker" printed on their pants while everyone else's uniforms are solid navy-blue scrubs and jumpsuits.

Although Captain James and the other jail administrators

made a decision to keep Triple J in the medical observation unit, he knew he could adjust.

"Tray Up, Trays Up Everybody," the female deputy calls out.

As she was passing Triple J's cell, she saw him sitting up in his chair.

"Mr. Johnson! You must be really hungry. You're up early." She said jokingly. "You know you didn't have to get out of bed. I would have got one of these guys to bring it in there to you," she continues speaking with the cell door ajar.

And that's exactly why I got up; he says to himself. *Because I felt that you would.*

His post-coma disability made it to where he didn't want to be around anyone foreign, especially in a jail cell. He was a little less concerned with medical staff but everyone else was not to be trusted.

"One thing that's good is that you're getting up on your own Mr. Johnson. You should try to get some rest also, I saw your name on the list for physical therapy today," the medical nurse says as she's following the breakfast train doing her morning rounds.

Triple J knew he had to get back right and get right quick especially since the Sergeant attacked him.

When the inmate worker walked around the cell door to hand him the food tray, Triple J eyed him up, getting a read on him. Non-threatening at all the elderly man nodded his head in a gentle gesture at the crime boss and continued moving. The officer closed the cell door as Triple J was opening the tray.

On top of his hardened grits was a folded note tapped with 'King Ape' written across the front of it. Cautiously examining the jailhouse kite, Triple J studied its handwriting, hoping to figure out who it could have come from. Briefly peeping out the large window, Triple J checks to see if the officer was away, before unraveling the folded note.

King Ape,

Today is definitely a great day for us Apes especially after watching the news these last few months getting nothing but some bull shit. I swear it's been hard on me, Ape. Nobody knew what was going on with you or how you even left. You know INMATE.com had all kinds of fucked up shit to say about you. Some folks was saying you fell down some stairs, then they say the green team beat you and threw you down some stairs. It's all kinds of stories going around on INMATE.com and things have been going Ape Shit since you left. We at war right now with the wolves after that lame ass niggas JT WOLF said you cooperate with the Feds. He claim you trying to take the family down. Nobody really know what to do everything fucked up so we all just split up. Back to how we started Grant Park Apes and them Washington Park Woosies. Them niggas ain't no wolves. Dogs are loyal and them niggas ain't it. I swear on the Ape God, I'm glad that you're back because I know if can't nobody get this shit right, King Ape can. I'm gone try to get down there and holla at you in medical. I swear we need you more than ever now Ape.

WE NEED YOU KING APE.

Ape Shit Flames...

As soon as Triple J finished reading the scribe he was startled by the voice of his grandfather.

"Your time is now," Baba Benji says as he speaks into the earpiece for the first time.

Hearing his Grandfather's voice Triple J knew then the time had come.

Shit Just Got 2 Real.

8

$\mathcal{E}$xhausted after physical therapy, Triple J returns back to his cell motivated to bounce back from his downfall. The physical pain he endured after therapy, couldn't compare to the mental suffering he felt knowing his wife and supposedly brother and business partner JT Wolf were messing around.

"The days to come before you are going to be rougher than you've ever experienced, but in the end, everything is going to work out for your good," Triple J's deceased grandfather's words replay in his head.

"I'm gone get right and show these lil fuckers why they should have never crossed me," Triple J says himself.

Triple J grabs his plastic urinal off the side of the bed and relieves himself. As he's getting ready to pull out his cell phone to call his attorney, a knock on the cell window caught his attention. Several deputies and two nurses stand in front of his cell.

"Hey Mr. Johnson," one of the white shirt sheriff deputies called out.

She was someone Triple J had not seen prior to that day. Although she was attractive, Triple J didn't see her as non-threatening. For all he knew, all of the staff in the Fulton Jail was corrupt in some way. He stared at her with a look on his face like he don't play the radio. "It's okay Mr. Johnson. We're not here to hurt you. I actually brought these nurses to help you get in your chair," she continued.

"Where are we going?" Triple J asked.

"You have an attorney visit," she told him.

Damn I was just about to call him, Triple J said to himself.

The deputies remain outside the cell once the door is open and the nurses go in. Assisting Triple J to his chair, they each grab one of his arms and walk him over. Safely seated, they roll him out the cell transporting the crime boss to his attorney visit.

Surrounded by several deputies, they go through the empty hallways' smooth sailing. Because Triple J's case was so high profile only a selected few staff members were allowed to make contact with him.

They get onto an elevator and it lowers to the second floor. While there transporting the crime boss butterflies began to swarm his stomach.

"The days to come before you are going to be rougher than you've ever experienced, but in the end, everything is going to work out for your good." Triple J again remembers his Baba's words.

This shit fucked up but it's going to work out for my good, he reminds himself as their rolling.

Off the elevators the transport team escorts the crime boss to the backside of central control, where the attorney booths are. One of the Deputies removes from his side pocket a ring of keys and unlocks the prisoner's side of the booth. The nurse that has been pushing the crime boss from his cell guides him into the attorney's booth, ~~and~~ no one says a word.

Locked in the 6x3 booth Triple J looks around as he waits for his attorney.

Damn I wish I had a coat or a blanket because it's cold in here, he says to himself as he looks around the booth for the air vent.

"Sheesh!"

According to inmate.com the low temperatures in the jail minimized the spread of common germs, similar to hospitals.

It's cool as Heaven down here, Triple J says to himself as he waits for his attorney to come in.

Stepping around the corner, wearing a blue plaid Giorgio Armani wool suit, was ATL's best dress attorney Torris J. Esquire. Carrying a leather black case with rose gold cufflinks hanging out the arm of his blazer, T.J. smiled when he saw his favorite client, thee James Johnson, Jr.

"Mr. Johnson!" He screams as he's taking a seat on a stool across from the crime boss. "I'm so glad to see you my friend," he continues as he puts his fist up to the separation glass.

Tired and weak, Triple J struggles to raise his hand to give his attorney an air dap, but he does enough to get the point across.

"It's good to see you too, TJ," Triple J replies.

"Man, for a second I thought we was going to lose you," TJ says.

"I see, and I'm glad to know you haven't moved on like some others," Triple J replies.

TJ looks down at his leather case as he's opening it because he too knew exactly what his client was talking about. Triple J's wife, Jessica stopped making attorney fee payments once doctors began questioning his recovery.

"Yes Mr. Johnson, I'm going to be here as long as I can," T.J replied.

At the time, Triple J didn't understand what he was saying but made sure to note it.

"As long as you can?" The crime boss asks his attorney.

"Well, you know we've come a long way together, but the monthly representation payments have stopped since your accident," TJ replies. "I don't know what's going on with your wife but she's stopped the legal funding...," Torris J says to him before everything goes silent in the crime boss's head.

Triple J clenches his fist and bangs it violently against the arm of his wheelchair.

Jessica was the sole beneficiary on all of his American accounts and had power of attorney in the event something happened to him.

"In this game of life, it's about making strategic moves. This shit is chess not checkers," Triple J's father James J told him before giving him his first kilo of heroine.

Cutting off his criminal defense funding, Jessica has gone too far. And that's when Triple J completely made up his mind, *The only woman I've ever loved has officially become the oops.*

Shit Just Got 2 Real.

9

*B*ack in his cell Triple J couldn't wait to get his phone.

I gotta call the bank. I know this bitch not gone take my money and leave me like this, he says to himself.

The Attorney visit wasn't valuable at all; they discussed little about the case. All Torris J came to say in so many words that if the money didn't start back flowing into his account, he would be removing himself from the case.

Fuck him to this money hungry black Jew fucker. He come in here with Armani suits on and shit that my money paid for and tell me when I need him most to go fuck myself.

Although he was emotionally scorn behind the betrayal from the only woman he's ever loved, Triple J knew he had to stay focused. With only seventeen percent battery charge left, on the burner phone Captain James brought him, Triple J made a call to the bank to check his account.

"Thank you for calling Atlanta's Best Bank. This is Sharon speaking," the woman says answering on the fourth ring.

Although it was still before twelve, she sounded like she'd been answering the phone all morning.

Triple J clears his throat before he begins to talk.

"Ahem, Good Morning Sharon this is James Johnson, Jr. I'm calling today in regards to my checking account balance. I had a…"

"Okay do you know your account number so I can pull you up," she says interrupting the crime boss.

"Em, not right of hand," Triple J replies.

"And you said your name is James Johnson, Jr. correct?" She asks.

"Yes"

"Okay for security purposes may I have the last four of your social,"

"1790," Triple J replies.

"Okay Mr. Johnson I'm looking here and it appears your checking account is negative three hundred seventy six dollars and fifty eight cents," she says breaking the news to him.

"What do you mean negative three hundred and seventy six dollars?" Triple J asks in a low but aggressive tone "I had over twenty thousand in my checking account a few months ago," he continues.

"Yes Mr. Johnson I see that here. Let me check on this for you," she says.

"Okay so what's my savings account balance then?" Triple J asks her, getting angry by the second.

"One second Mr. Johnson," she says to him.

Triple J looks down at his free hand and tries to steady the anxiety racing through them. The uncontrollable shivers began to get so severe that Triple J began biting his nails wondering if he would get through.

The last balance he remembered having was eleven million dollars in his personal savings, and fifty-four million dollars combined in both his business checking and savings accounts. Jessica leaving him for his homie was already depressing. If she's worked the other one on him, taken all of his money, Triple J's financial future could possibly be below the poverty level.

"Hey Mr. Johnson are you still there," the female banker asks after returning to the call.

"Yes! I'm here," he replies.

"Okay, so there was some fraudulent activity detected to your account and before I can move any further you would have to come into the bank with two forms of identification," the banker tells him.

"I'm actually in the middle of the jungle," Triple J says to the banker, "and I don't know when I'll be able to come inside," he continues.

"Well because our security department has detected fraudulent activity to this account, I won't be able to give you any additional information in regards to this account. Thank you for choosing Atlanta's Best Bank. My name is Sharon. Please enjoy the rest of this great day and make sure to use bug spray," she said sarcastically before ending the call.

Shit Just Got 2 Real

10

*S*ince waking from the coma, Triple J started to get the feeling that everybody who disliked him that has been hiding in the nooks and crannies were starting to come out now.

They think this disability gone last forever, but I'm gone bounce back. I'm gone bounce back harder than anyone has ever seen, he tells himself.

One thing to be true about the underworld, if you're a boss that's just something that will never change. Triple J's a real one with generational family ties. The long-term relationships their families have are so secure that a double blade sword wouldn't be able to sever them.

Loyalty over royalties, is the saying that true bosses live by. Although someone had put out rumors of him cooperating with authorities, the real ones knew that not to be true. Connected with heads all across the country he knew they had all kinds of connections on the inside, local, state and federal. Before he would ever get to make a statement, word would have got to them and he would be dead. Shit gets 2 real in the underworld.

With only 6 percent charge on his phone, Triple J knew it was time to call the elders. Johnny Burrell, Triple J's Godfather and life time best friend to his father, is an Atlanta Street legend with ties around the world. The streets gave Johnny Burrell the moniker of "Rev" due to his influential voice in the community. For Triple J he's always simply been Uncle BJ.

As the phone began ringing butterflies swarmed his stomach. Triple J knew the severity of making this call and once he asked for this favor there was no coming back.

"Yeah," his Godfather answers in his raspy voice.

"Uncle BJ!" Triple J says knowing he was the only one that called him that.

"Hey Son, I see you got one of them thangs," he replies.

"Yeah, you know it don't take long for niggas like us," Triple J replies.

"I hear ya son. You just like me and your daddy. I guess that ol saying is true, the apple don't fall too far from the tree," he says.

"Naw it don't Unc."

"Well I know you ain't call just to check on the old man. Give it to me raw," his Godfather asked of him.

"The lawyer came to see me today saying the payments stopped," Triple J tells him.

"Ah hell! That's all them ol jew boys want mo money and mo money. Aite send ya daddy by here to take care of that," Unc replies.

"That's not it," Triple J tells him. "Ever since this accident everybody been switching up," he continues.

"Yeah I heard. I told you them ol politics folks ain't to be trusted and you married the damn daughter," his Godfather replies. "Let me know what you wanna do?"

"Excommunicated," Triple J replies, referring to his wife Jessica and JT Wolf.

Excommunication is when one has been removed from the family and all ties are cut with that person. Because everyone knew that Jessica was Triple J's wife and JT Wolf was his business partner, they were able to conduct business on his behalf up until now. Now that they've been removed from the underworld no one is allowed to conduct any business with either of them, not even conversation.

"Taken care of," Triple J's God Father replies before the phone goes dead.

For the rest of that evening Triple J went through the motions of incarceration, pill call, chow call, count time and shift change. Since severing ties with his wife and JT Wolf, King Ape knew the Ape ship needed its original captain to get things steering again.

I swear we need you more than ever now Ape, Triple J thought as he remembered Flamez words.

Never minding any more of the negativity, Triple J channeled all his energy towards bettering the Ape family. The first thing he knew he had to do was get back right.

Climbing off the bunk, Triple J rolls to the floor falling to his hands. Although the medical staff told him to take it easy, the crime boss just couldn't lay down. He had a family to feed.

Pushing himself on his road to recovery, he fights to get his strength back.

They say scar tissue is the best tissue, Triple J says self-motivating himself as he begins doing push ups.

Struggling to push his own body weight up Triple J fights the burn because he knew this was something that had to be done. Down and up, he goes locking his arms each time he comes up. On the down he uses the floor to bounce his chest off and springs back up.

After completing several sets of push-ups Triple J then turns over to work his core area, remembering that strong core is what keeps the body together. Placing his fingertips around the temple area of his head, Triple J lifts his knees to his chest and begins the crunch exercise.

"Arrh!" He screams after his second set of 8.

Feeling the burn, he continues to motivate himself saying, "I gotta get back right"

Continuing to push himself he then moves forward with flutter kicks, scissors and Russian abdominal twists.

"You got it grandson!" Triple J hears the voice of the ancestors speaking to him.

The enthusiastic tone in his grandfather's voice let him know that he was proud. After a few sets of leg strength-ening exercises, Triple J finally calls it quits.

It seemed like his timing couldn't have been more perfect. As soon as he finished his workout it was 4pm, an hour after the shift changed. Usually, showers were conducted early in the day on the medical floor, but due to the staff shortages they were carried out later in the day.

Never minding the door sheets, Deputy Harris also known as Officer Friendly unlocks all the cells in MOU for showers.

"Alright now, I'm giving y'all a hour and ten minutes exactly to take showers. Everybody in here that can walk help these cripples in these wheelchairs," he says, making a joke. "Get them some hot water for their buckets and if anybody need some help get them a nurse. I'll be back to lock y'all down in one hour and nine minutes," he finished as he looked at his watch.

Deputy Harris, a veteran Deputy with the Sheriff department, was the coolest jailer to ever walk inside of Fulton jail walls. Rumor was he had a nephew on the fifth floor named Spud that he looked out for here and there, keeping him with free world vending items. Inmate.com reported that other relatives of Deputy Harris passed through the system and he looked out for them too. Seeing members of his family incarcerated gave him an open eye for the job causing him to treat everyone with respect. Because he had a reputation for being so cool Jail administrators made sure to keep him working the medical floor where there wasn't much going on.

Triple J knew he needed to clean himself since he'd been sweating but he didn't want to be around anyone in his physical state. Although he was handicap, he had a murderous reputation everyone knew about.

Sitting down in his wheelchair, Triple J grabs his water tub and lays it on his lap. He clutches a makeshift knife he filed from a crutch handle in his right hand as he rolls out his cell. As he's rolling towards the shower area, he sees a ghost walking down the range towards him.

Damn, I thought this mother fucker was dead, Triple J says before someone pushes the back of his chair.

Shit Just Got 2 Real

11

The murder game was nothing new to a crime boss like Triple J, clearly being that he was in the Fulton Jail awaiting trial on the charge. But like others, in the mafia, Triple J's preferred weapon of choice was the .38 snub nose revolver. It was easy to conceal giving you the ability to get up close and personal, when finishing a job. Its street moniker is the shell catcher because of it holds on to spent casings, making it difficult for law enforcement to identify a murder weapon. The up close and personal experience was nothing to the crime boss but it was when Triple J witnessed it on the inside.

During his first 24 hours of incarceration, while the breakfast trays were being passed out, shit got real. Hearing speculative reasons after, Triple J's neighbor was ambushed in the chow line and consequently eaten for breakfast by a group of hyenas with knives. The poor guy was stabbed so many times and left for dead on the floor at least until the emergency response team marched in blasting their guns. Triple J thought he witnessed that man take his last breath.

Standing before him was the man he swore had died. Unaware of his mental state, Triple J used caution clutching his knife under the water tub. Even though he and the man never had words he still had to be on point. Fact of the matter remains; Triple J was charged after with the assault after a victim statement was made alleging him to be the perpetrator at the time. Thanks to a surveillance review by the jail's staff, charges were later dropped, but still Triple J didn't know what the victims mind set was.

Pulling his knife from under the bucket's lip, Triple J turns in his chair to see who's pushing him. Viewing the knife in Triple J's hand he released the chair and took a quick step back.

"OG Big Boo told us to watch your back down here," the young guy says quickly with medical gauze taped to the right side of his face.

You can't even protect yourself how you gone watch my back? Triple J says to himself.

"How can you push my chair and watch my back at the same time?" Triple J asks the young man in a stern tone. "You suppose to stand back and pay attention to what's going on around me, not up on me," he finishes.

Triple J could tell all the young man wanted to be was a help to the crime boss, so he invited him to walk with him.

"I appreciate you young man. Do you mind carrying this water tub for me?" He asks the young man.

"Hell naw I don't mind. I got you King Ape," the young fella says excitedly.

His entire facial expression changed as he proceeded with the crime boss. Triple J could sense his nervousness but still gave the guy the opportunity to learn from him.

"What do they call you?" Triple J asks knowing most guys incarcerated go by monikers.

"They call me Jew Boy!" He says excitedly.

"Jew Boy? How you get that name?" Triple J asks.

"It's always been a dream of mine to become a lawyer. I feel like God put me here for a reason because I've been able to help a lot of guys find loopholes in their cases," Jew Boy says.

"That's what's up. So how did you end up in here?" Triple J asks.

Jew Boy lays his head down and shakes it from side to side before he answers.

"This bitch ass nigga my mama married kept beating on her and one day I just got tired of it. He was in the room beating and kicking her, so I kicked the door, stabbed him in the neck twice with a butcher knife and bitch bleed out like a hog," Jew Boy says, with menacing eyes and not a hint of remorse in his voice.

Triple J could understand his reasoning for reacting violently, even though he didn't grow up with a mother.

If anybody fucked with pop, he said to himself, *they would've probably gotten it a lot worse.*

Jew Boy didn't seem like a bad kid. He spoke with mannerism and pronounced his words correctly. Had he not been in the same uniform as Triple J, he could have passed for a young attorney.

Eager to know what happened to his face Triple J finally asked.

"You seem like a good kid. And I hate you got caught up in your mama shit," Triple J says while shaking his head. "I'm just confused. You look healthy other than that gauze on your face. What's got you down here?" Triple J asks, referring to his MOU status.

Jew Boy energy changes and Triple J can feel the difference as he touches his face.

"We were all laughing at the entertainment from two of my brothers debating over the Georgia and Alabama game. Everything was cool until one of them whipped out his banger. Both of them brought out the knives and went under the stairs. You know away from the camera view," Jew Boy pauses. "As soon as they got back there that's when shit got 2 real. I wasn't gone let them go out like that so I tried stopping the shit. Knives went to swinging right as I got there and Wham! I got hit in the face. The blade punctured my jaw and came out my mouth. Doctors said had my mouth been closed at the time I would have been in worse shape than this," Jew Boy finishes.

"Damn!" Was all Triple J could say to that.

"Yeah, it's fucked up but hey look at the bright side. If that hadn't happened then I wouldn't be down here to meet the Honorable Triple J," Jew Boy says, patronizing the crime boss.

"Yeah.. but you ain't gotta do all that Honorable shit," Triple J says with a smirk on his face.

"Let's be honest you already know you're the talk of the town and whenever your name comes up it's like a folktale. Legend says," Jew Boy continues before they both burst into laughter.

"I preshate you man," Triple J says as he's laughing.

Finally reaching the rear of the unit Jew Boy goes into a utility closet to get warm water for Triple J's water bucket. As he's filling the bucket the guy from upstairs heads towards him again.

"What's up with you?" Triple J asks the weirdo.

"Whatever you want to be up," he answers incorrectly.

Triple J clutches his knife but before he can react Jew Boy comes out of the closet.

"I don't give a fuck what kind of problem you thought you had with the Big Homie but whatever it was it's dead on Red," Jew Boy says as he's walking up on him.

"You can get it...," the guy starts to say before he's dashed with the warm water Jew Boy was carrying.

Triple J knew the bum buster wasn't about that life remembering how he folded on the 7th floor, but Jew Boy had already pooped it off. Feeding him the hot water before quickly closing the distance between them. Blinded by the water the man didn't see it coming but most definitely felt it when Jew Boy smashed his fist in his gut. Working his hands like a professional prize fighter Jew Boy folded him over and quickly picked him up with a hard uppercut under the chin.

Crunch! His chin sounds off from the hard blow to his chin.

"Whoa!" Triple J screams halting the raging man as he's about to fall on top of him. "He get the picture. Let's roll out." Triple J says with authority.

Looking back at the crime boss with murder in his eyes Jew Boy halts even though he wants to finish. Snatching the water bucket from the floor he returns back to the closet and fills the water tub for the crime boss.

Staring at the unconscious man as he lays stiffened on the floor, Triple J starts to think. *Where does the animosity come from with this man? I don't even know him.* Triple J reminds himself. *Whatever it is I hope it's over with now.*

Filling the water tub enough so that the crime boss can clean himself up, Jew Boy exits the closet in silence and they head back towards the crime boss's cell. Other than his face filled with sweat from the quick physical altercation, they continue as if nothing ever happened. When they reach the room, Jew Boy set the bucket on the wall across from Triple J's bed.

"Go ahead and get yourself together I'm gone stand out here," Jew Boy says to the crime boss before he stands guard.

"Preshate ya," Triple J replies.

Oblivious to why they were beefing, Triple J wondered why the lil dude had an issue with him.

It can't be nothing other than he thought I either busted him up on the floor or told them to do it. Whichever one I hope it's over with.

Right as Triple J finishes and gets ready to chop it up a little more with Jew Boy before lockdown, the slide doors to MOU could be heard opening. Walking in deep was the jail's goon crew, The Green Team. They approach Triple J's cell and make contact with his outside security first.

"Turn around!" One of them yells at Jew Boy.

Before he can comply three of them grab him and slam him into the window of Triple J's cell.

Staring in at the crime boss as they handcuffed him, they both knew what it was.

Shit Just Got 2 Real.

12

*T*he way *The Green Team marched in and snatched the young Jew Boy wasn't fair*, Triple J thought but he knew that was all a part of being incarcerated.

"Their way of showing who's in charge," he reminds himself.

It was cool for them but costly for the crime boss. In the Fulton Jail there was an unwritten rule that if your homie goes to lock up, you make sure they have what they need; snacks, hygiene, and other commissary items. If Triple J was still up on the 7th floor, where segregation is, he would have made sure the young gunna had plenty, cell phone and all.

Although this incident was unexpected and Triple J knew that Captain James would be coming to see him soon. He couldn't just leave the youngin in lock up so he was prepared to use his Trump card.

As he was scheming on his next move the devil himself walked up to his cell.

"Damn, you just can't stay low key, can you?" Captain James asks after he unlocks his cell and walks in. "Why is it that you and Antonio Coleman keep having problems. First it was upstairs, now it's down here, where you're supposed to be chilling. You know what, now I'm beginning to think it's more to this situation," Captain James says.

"I was exonerated of the last situation, if I'm not mistaken," Triple J reminds the Captain.

"Come on with the bull shit! The man's jaw is broken," Captain James screams upset.

"You did that! Knowing good and got damn well there was an issue in the past," Triple J says.

"Oh so this is retaliation for him snitching?" The Captain asks.

"Remember the last issue, you asked me to let you handle it. You know how I solve problems, Captain James. Please remember who you're talking to," Triple J reminds the Captain.

Captain James knew the power of the crime boss. *If Triple J wanted to get something done it would have been handled quietly and professionally.* After putting two and two together Captain James reached a conclusion

Incident Report

"On the above date injured inmate, Antonio Colman JID 1005431980 was involved in a physical altercation. Upon my investigation, the inmate above was deemed the aggressor by approaching two other inmates with ill intentions. During the altercation the above inmate sustained multiple injuries that were documented by medical as non-life threatening. Neither of the parties involved requested to press outside charges, none will be brought against either or the inmates involved," his report said.

Before leaving Triple J's cell, Captain James left the crime boss with a token. A brand new touch screen iPhone with two charging battery packs. Captain James knew the crime boss wasn't in the best position to get them back up and going so he made sure the crime boss had what he needed to stay connected with the outside world.

As the Captain departed Triple J thanked him.

"Gratitude, Sir."

Now that he was back on deck with a touch screen phone and front face camera the first person he thought to call was his wife Jessica. They stayed in contact before his injury, but now that no longer exists.

As he sits there alone Triple begins to look back over the situation and is immediately reminded of how serious things can get on the inside. Had he not stopped Jew Boy, chances are he would have beaten that man through the floor.

This my lil nigga, Triple J says excited validating Jew Boy as family now.

Seeing so much of the young man in himself, Triple J begins to think what it would be like to have a son. *Damn I got Jessica and this flight attendant pregnant,* he's reminded. *Ain't no way she trying me like this,* Triple J says to himself. *I know she not fucking this nigga with my baby in her.*

Right before he gets ready to power on the cell phone Captain James brought him, he gets another unexpected visit.

"Mail Call! Mail Call! Mail Call!" A female officer screams as she enters MOU. Her voice was different from the last mail lady Triple J remembered.

Standing outside of his cell she uses the ring of keys to unlock his cell. "Mr. Johnson you have a lot of mail including legal mail I'm going to need you to sign for some of this" she says.

"Where is Ms. Grant?" Triple J asks looking for the last mail lady.

"Here I go Mr. Johnson," Officer Grant says as she approaches pushing a silver rolling cart.

"What's up Lady," he says excited to see her.

Since coming out of the coma it's been a real road to recovery. Doctors said his recovery would be much easier with familiar people around.

She still looks the same, he says to himself.

On the low Triple J had a crush on Officer Grant. She wasn't the best looking woman he's ever seen but she did have that sex appeal that made her so attractive. As he stares at her, Aqyila's song "Vibe for me," starts playing in his head.

"It's the vibe for me, it's the vibe for me," the beautiful voice sang.

The other officer hands Triple J a black hard back book.

"Sign your name next to the x," she says.

"And I gotta give you all this too," Ms. Grant says, passing Triple J 3 large bundles of rubber-band letters.

"All this for me?" He asks.

"Yes! Most of it is cards and letters fans sent you," Ms. Grant says.

"Thank you," Triple J says again as he's receiving the last letters.

At the hospital he felt as if no one cared about him, especially after the devastating call to his wife.

Laying all the letters on his bed Triple J began to organize them. One by one he reads off the names separating the ones he knew from the ones that didn't ring a bell.

Throughout the whole stack only one letter was from

Jessica. She'd written him and for some strange reason he felt as though reading it would give him some closure.

Dear James,

The man I married was an impressive black man that stood tall and firm on loyalty. The man I married gave me his word that he would never leave nor forsake me. James how could you sleep with all of these random whores passing out what's supposed to be ours. Just so you know I know about the Airplane bitch she contacted me and let me know about y'all little baster baby. You said you would never hurt me and this shit is just something you can never return from. For all I care now you're dead to me so our vows "till death do us 'part" is now. I ain't got shit for you and I don't want shit from you, not even your child. This little shit coming up out of me tomorrow....

Closing his eyes Triple J stops reading the letter as tears begin to trail down the side of his face.

Shit Just Got 2 Real

13

Several days went by without the crime boss coming out of his cell. Refusing physical therapy and everything else he could do on the inside; Triple J began contemplating suicide. It seemed like everything tragic that could happen to a person was happening to him and it wouldn't end.

Who would have ever thought this would be my life? He asks himself.

Captain James stopped by several times to speak with him but Triple J just couldn't talk, depression had taken over his life. Seeing that he couldn't get through to the crime boss Captain James was left with no other choice. He sent in the ultimate weapon, Lt Rodgers.

Since returning from the hospital she'd been waiting for the green light. Wasting no time, she rushed to the cell of Triple J taking the keys from the floor officer. With her big pretty smile on her face, she unlocked his cell and walked in with authority.

"Get the fuck up! I need to have a word with you in my office," she says blushing between her teeth.

Triple J looks at her for a few seconds scanning her up and down with a mug in his face like they were beefing.

"Don't look at me like! that! I said get up motha fucka," she continues placing her right hand on her duty belt.

Not in the mood for any company or conversation, he continued to mug her but couldn't let her get off talking to him like that.

"Who you think you is?" He asked her with a serious tone in his voice.

"Who am I? Who am I?" She asks while patting her hands on her crouch. I'm Lieutenant Mother Fucking Rogers and I said get the fuck up," she continues.

Looking down at her crotch area, Triple J thinks about their last fuck festival. Honestly it was a bundle of joy but depressing at the same time. On that same day his wife Jessica busted him and found out about their fling.

Not really feeling the play, Triple J played along because he did want to feel better.

I gotta shake this depression shit and she think she slick coming up here with these store call pants?? on," he says to himself. *"I'll be damned if I let her get away,"* he continues.

Climbing off the bed, Triple J rolls over onto his wheel-chair. Lieutenant Rodgers pulls out her handcuffs because the jail's policy requires him to be in hand restraints to leave the floor. Standing in front of him she secures his hands, rubbing her dripping vagina against' his hands. Triple J smiles and bites his bottom lip.

She already dripping! He says feeling the moisture on the front of her pants.

As they head down to her office Lt Rodgers starts singing *Nice & Slow* by Usher while there alone on the elevator.

"I'm gonna take you to a place nice and quiet," she sings before bursting out into a laugh.

Triple J looks back at her blushing because he knew that shit was about to get 2 real.

"Who's gone freak you like me?" He fires back at her in his Keith Sweat voice.

"Nobody!" She says joining in helping him complete the *Nobody* song.

They both had a natural connection and synchronized well together. Lt Rodgers never gave a care about his marriage; he was hers from the start. Now that Triple J was unofficially divorce, he didn't care either.

Rolling him into her office Lt Rodgers stops the crime boss in front of her desk.

"I don't give a damn about this wheel chair shit," she tells him "You know the rules. So don't come down here with that bull shit. I better get mines before you get yours," she continues.

Triple J smiles because her shit talking was different.

"I see this police shit dun ran to your head," he says referring to her attempts at bedroom dominance. "I'm bout to break all this shit down. I wear the Big drawl's" he continues beating on his chest like an Ape as he stands from his chair.

"Okay! Big Zaddy," She says blushing while biting down on her finger..

He grabs her by the belt and pulls her to him.

"You know you bae right?" He asks her.

"Am I?" She questions him.

Triple J says no more unfastening her pants and pulls them down slowly.

"Take this shit off me," he says referring to the handcuffs she has him in.

"Don't fuck up my fantasy," she says to him.

"I said take them off," he spits back with dominance in his voice.

"Yes! Big Zaddy," she quickly responds, bending down in front of him grabbing her handcuff key from her pants pocket.

Once she removes the cuffs Triple J pops it off. Grabbing her by the neck he begins kissing her. Running his hand down her curvature, he gets a full erection while wrestling with her warm tongue.

"Damn I miss this pussy," he says as he sits Lt Rodgers down at the edge of her desk.

"You know you bae right?" He asks her again.

"Show me," she replies with an attitude.

Dropping to his knees Triple J buries his head between her legs running his tongue down the middle of her thigh. He begins kissing her Pune Pie, orally massaging her vagina with his tongue. As soon as he starts sucking softly on her clit she screams.

"Owe, owe, owe!" she says laying her head back on the desk with sporadic jerks running through her body. "Why you doing this to me?" She asks.

Triple J smiles as he continues to please her.

Lt. Rodgers rests her hand on Triple J's head and begins to grind on his face, moving her hips in a full 360 motion.

"You know you bae right?" He asks again with his face still stuffed in her vagina.

"So you say," she continues her sarcasm as he begins fondling her breast.

Again, Triple J smiles before he gets sloppy with the top.

Setting off all kinds of sexual vibrations in her body as he orally manipulates her vagina, Lt Rodgers goes crazy as her body waves like an ocean.

"Ohh Fuck," she screams as she begins to ejaculate.

Knowing he hit the bullseye Triple J goes harder with the top causing her to scream louder.

"Bae, Bae, Bae, Bae, Bae!" She repeats rapidly. "I'm your bae, I'm your bae!" She continues.

Continuing to please her as she explodes, Triple J makes her go Koo Koo crazy.

"Okay, okay! I'm your Bae, I'm your Bae," she screams as she struggles to lift his head away.

Smiling with a sinister look on his face as he lifts up and finalizes his victory with a fist pump.

"I told you I was gone get that mouth," he says to her before beating on his chest.

She mugs him before she crashes on the desk in fatigue.

Shit Just Got 2 Real.

14

What a joyful moment it was for the Lieutenant and the ATL crime boss. Although he wasn't at full strength, he laid down the pipe pleasing her more with every stroke. Collectively, moments like these were the ones neither of them wanted to end.

"You gotta get out of here," she says referring to his incarceration as she wheels him back to his cell.

"I most definitely agree with you," he replies.

Educated in so many areas of life, due to his love for reading books, Triple J slowly began to remember one science journal he'd read.

During the post sex periods the manifestation gateway is open for business.

When Lt Rodgers began speaking about his release, he used that time to tap into the portal and fill it with manifestation vibrations.

There is nothing for me being locked inside these four walls. Even though she wants me to be released for this dick, I got real work to do.

As he was thinking about getting out, he started to think about his lil homies locked on the inside.

I'm ready to go but I can't be selfish. These young men have laid their lives on the line for something we started. They need their commander. A real leader who's going to educate them and help them make it to the next level of life. Since there was no more ANW I gotta come up with another name for us.

Lt Rodgers continues with her sexual advances but Triple J couldn't think about that anymore. It was time for him to live out his purpose.

We got business to handle.

As they're entering the medical unit, Triple J sees that his cell door is ajar with an officer standing in front. A few items can be seen on the outside and movement can be heard on the inside. Immediately Triple J thinks the worst.

Damn, they shaking down my cell.

"What y'all doing in this cell?" Lt Rodgers asks the floor officer as they approach.

"Um, yes ma'am! Captain James called and instructed me to move inmate Cochran to this cell," the floor officer answers hesitantly.

Triple J didn't know an inmate Cochran and didn't care for any cellmate at this time. As Lt Rodgers continued to push him closer to his cell he began to think rapidly.

What the hell does Captain James have up his sleeve now. He got to know ain't no anybody coming up there with me.

At his cell's entrance, Triple J sees an unshaven young face displaying all 32 teeth through his smile. Like the deadly respiratory coronavirus infection, Triple J was instantly infected by the young smile, and the hugest smile erupts across his face.

"Heyy manee!" The young gun says cooler than Rollie Click Chris.

Depression had begun to kick the Crime Bosses ass but now he was so happy to have his lil homie Jew Boy back.

Shit Just Got 2 Real

15

*H*aving the young soul around, Jew Boy, felt necessary for the recovering crime boss and his mental health. The two of them shared their incarcerated space together, like a little brother big brother duo, in their mothers home.

More motivated than before they turned their 9x12 jail cell into a fitness gym. Starting off strong they hit two a day workouts. Morning and evening push-ups, sit ups and squats regiments. Using a deck of playing cards the count changed each set. Pulling three cards at a time the numbers were added together and the results were their amount of reps to do. Although the crime boss was physically weaker because of his accident, he was mentally strong pushing himself harder each set that they did.

The two a day workouts went well and it really did speed up Triple J's recovery. Shocking the physical therapists during therapy sessions, they were surprised at how quick he regained his mobility. There was no way Triple J would allow himself to be defeated, so he continued to kick depression's ass like a member of the Bully Breed Familia.

Over time, Triple J and Jew Boy built a brotherly bond, giving the both of them an incarcerated comfort. No one wanted to feel alone and right now they were all they had.

I'll thank him later, Triple J makes a mental note as he thinks about the move Captain James made, putting the vibrant soul in his cell.

Ever since the depressing letter came in from Triple J's wife Jessica, he hadn't read any more mail. A large pile began to form under his bed and it continued to grow.

"They love you out there, Big Bruh," Jew Boy says as another wave of mail comes in. "I wish I was like you and I had people to write me," he continued.

"You do," Triple J says to him, feeding the young man some confidence.

"That pile under the bunk over there is all yours now and every other piece of mail that comes through the door belongs to you Lil bruh."

"On everything?" Jew Boys asks.

"On everything," Triple J continues.

Nothing was more soothing for the crime boss than to see the excitement on the young man's face when he was gifted. Everything he'd received from the crime boss he took good care of and cherished it like it was his last.

He gone be alright, Triple J thought to himself. *And I'm gone make sure of that.*

Now that he was out of the coma and doing better, Triple J had to connect with the ANW subchapter heads. There was a fire, JT Wolf and his wife Jessica set, within the organization that needed immediate containment. After several messages with the tops on an encrypted messaging app,

Triple J found out that many were worried about the future of the crime family. Word traveled across the country to other members about the severing of ANW's original Atlanta Chapter and no one knew what to expect next. Looking to the Boss for reassurance Triple J had to organize a conference call.

Because he shared the cell with an outsider, Triple J had to be extremely cautious when communicating out loud. Although Jew Boy was like his little brother now, JT Wolf was also once upon a time ago.

Nobody is to be trusted as much, Triple J says to himself. *Whatever you do you never let your right hand know what your left is doing*, he remembers his father's words.

There was a one hour window for him to set up the conference call while they ran showers. OG Big Boo assigned the young Jew Boy to protect him and that's what Triple J was going to use him for during tomorrow's shower call.

I gotta bring the family back together, he says to himself. *It's a lot that's going to change. A lot! All for the better. All for the better.* He repeats as he falls asleep.

ANW was his family. Although there were some changes going on with the Apes and Wolves, he wanted to keep the three-letter acronym.

Visiting him in his sleep, Triple J's grandfather reached out to have a word with the crime boss.

"*My Son,*

You've traveled a considerable distance down the road of recovery and we're proud of you. Many opposed your transition and expect for you to be weak when you return. They've prayed, wished and hoped for every negative result. In a way, they're going to get what they seek in your temporary defeat, but now we unleash the beast. The time has come for you to go Ape Shit, how you and your boys say it. Everyone is expecting you to take the fall but you're going to give rise above all levels and show them different. The trading of illegal substances must be abolished from the orga-nization. You'll introduce the guys to the Wall Street hustle. Educating them in Foreign Exchange, cryptos and all the new things like NFT's. You'll breed ghetto educators teaching thugs about bullish and bearish markets. Your digital transition will be the breakthrough for many of the Apes suffering from systematic oppression. You're going to make them respect the Ape's grandson. You're going to be great. There's been bulls and bears on Wall Street but now it's time to introduce them to the Apes."

Triple J opens his eyes and smiles as he stares at the seasoned mustard stains on the roof of his jail cell. As he prepares himself to lead tomorrow's conference call.

It's time to introduce the guys to the new and important ANW. The Ape's on Wall-street.

Shit Just Got 2 Real.

16

*R*ising from the bed earlier than usual, Triple J dives into his A.M. workout alone. His youthful cell mate and work out partner Jew Boy, knew there was something serious, on the mind of the crime boss because normally they exercised together.

"What's up Big Homie? You riding without me now?" Jew Boy asks in his morning voice.

"Naw! It's not like that. A lot's going on right now Lil Homie and I really couldn't sleep," Triple J says, tapping his finger twice on his temple. "Plus, I didn't wanna wake you all extra early," he continues.

"We got all day to sleep Big Homie if I need to. You know our routine every morning is to bang out these push-ups. That's what I'm looking forward to every morning. Helping you get back all of your strength."

The words of the young man were touching and Triple J knew them to be true. He had the utmost respect for the crime boss and wished nothing but the best for him on his road to recovery.

Their bond had become tight since they were now cellies. On the inside they were brothers, but Triple J's past made him keep a certain distance with the young gunna.

I can't let him get close; he reminds himself.

"That's my bad Big Brother. I don't ever want you to think that I don't appreciate you because I definitely do. I just woke up with a lot of pent up and I needed to work it off," the crime boss reiterates.

"Respectfully," the young Jew Boy replies. "But why did you call me your Big Brother and you're older than me."

Triple J smiles as he stands from the floor.

Physically he's come a long way since waking from the coma. Doctors projected it would be at least six months before Triple J would be able to stand on his own, but he was already doing it in way less time.

"What's a big brother? Someone you look up to and learn from, right?" Jew Boy shakes his head up and down in agreement. "Every day you teach me something new Big Brother. These thugs I can incorporate into my life forever," Triple J says as he reaches out his hands and daps the young man. "I see nothing but greatness in you. Financial success and freedom all over your life. You're going to have way more than what I've ever achieved and that's why I look up to you, Big Brother." He finishes.

"You really see that?" Jew Boy asks as a huge smile erupts across his face.

"Definitely! I see you being one of the greatest attorneys to come through Georgia." The crime boss continues. "You know it's in your Bloodline. You're a Cochran just like the G.O.A.T, Mr. Johnnie Cochran Esq."

Triple J had plans for today's family meeting to exclude

the young man, but there were so many indications that reversed those plans.

Triple J concluded that the young Jew Boy was going to be groomed as his liaison, especially now that ANW was headed in a different direction.

Great men like Jew Boy are needed in this family, Triple J thought.

As he prepared himself for the transition, Triple J's hypothesis was that many of the guys would be reluctant against the new direction of the organization. Regardless of what they choose to do, ANW was for now for the future business leaders of the world instead of drug dealers.

"I'm going to need you in 5 minutes," Triple J says.

"I'm here. I ain't going nowhere," Jew Boy replies humorously.

"It's an important call I have to make today," Triple J begins before Jew Boy interrupts.

"Say no more. I'm gone step out and watch for 12," he quickly replies.

"Naw I need you in here with me," he says, causing the young man's face to light up in amazement, "I'm taking ANW in a different direction and I want you to be a part of it. We've had to sever ties with the Wolves so I've been thinking what's the next move. This little time incarcerated has shown me a different side to this street shit. For the ones that wanna go in this new direction with me, I'm gone make sure they see a ticket by the end of the year."

Jew Boy's eyes went roaming, as he thought about what Triple J was saying, *A ticket by the end of the year? Damn, That's a whole million dollars.*

"My plan is to keep the ANW acronyms but give it a twist. Instead of being the Apes and Wolves we're the Apes on Wall street?" Triple J says showing Jew Boy a sheet of paper with the capital spelling highlighted.

Turning his head from left to right in disagreement Jew Boy says, "That ain't it, Big Homie. If you're going to do something new, it needs to be new. Even if it's the same crew."

Triple J began to think about what he was saying but no other name came to mind.

"What's that name your homie called you that one time, The Executive Homeboy or something like that?" Jew Boy asked.

Triple J laughs.

"Yeah, that's what Bugg called me his executive homeboy,"

"Well think about this. Since your building millionaires, how about you drop the ANW name altogether. You don't want people associating the new group with criminal activity. I think you should go with something like, The Executive Homies Inc. It has a louder ring than Apes on Wall Street. You feel me? White folks gone get scared to work with you. 'Calling a black boy an Ape, wow! I thought that was racist.

We maybe should stay away from these guys. I don't want to lose everything my family has worked so hard for just to lose it over some racist antics," Jew Boy mocks in his white voice.

That does make perfect sense, Triple J says putting his hand on his head in thought.

"Apes on Wall Street sounds like you're planning to crash the stock market, with some jungle boys," Jew Boy continues to joke.

Triple J laughs louder this time, but honestly, he knew Jew Boy was right.

"You definitely have a great analytical point that I wasn't

thinking about. The Executive Homies will have a more polysemous uniqueness to it, especially since we're going from rags to riches."

"Naw, Bunks to Billions," Jew Boy corrects him with a face full of excitement.

Neither were prepared for this next move, but both agreed it was major. Staring at one other with smiles from ear to ear they both knew that then,

Shit Just Got 2 Real.

17

*T*he mass message was sent out for a 3p.m. conference call. Neither of the eight leaders knew what the call was about, but everyone knew they had to be on there, even with the short notice. A lot was going on with the ANW family and mixed emotions were pent up towards the crime boss, especially with the snitch shit going around on his name.

It was a lot but Triple J was their savior. Him being out of the picture was a huge let down for many of the guys, but knowing his position he felt it was only right to give these men an opportunity to transition with him.

"Apes up Everybody," he begins the call greeting the guys.

"Apes Up!" They respond synchronized.

"I would like to first apologize for the short notice given in regards to this well overdue family meeting. Today, I plan to clear the airwaves of the few discrepancies I've heard lingering around. Despite the unexpected displacement my involuntary vacation has caused, we've still been able to maintain our business and I give the most thanks to you guys. We are the pillars of this organization and it's important that we keep the family together. From the time I stepped off the porch to these troubling days of incarceration, I've always been about raising the bar. The merger we made with the Wolves was done in good faith, but unfortunately there has been a severance amongst us. "Ne—ver di—d I want it to come," Triple J says pausing on his words, "to this but it has." This short period of time incarcerated has taught me a lot. When we started the Grant Park Apes we were poor little boys in the ghetto just trying to make it. I never imagined we would grow and become as big as we did. The news and police didn't call us a gang, they labeled us a crime family," Triple J laughs out loud. "We've overcome every obstacle the game has brought against us. When they brought smoke, we made sure to come out on top when it cleared. It's been a journey for all of us. A journey that we've mostly controlled. I've met so many of our lil homies in here and it's shown me a lot. Law enforcement is cracking down on us and before we lose everything we have to save what we have. ANW has split and we've been known to go Ape Shit. That's how we started but is that how we're supposed to end? I don't think so. We've become much greater men, business leaders and entrepreneurs so instead of identifying ourselves as Apes any longer, we are now, The Executive Homies," Triple J says as he finishes.

There was a brief silence on the call before one of his Lieutenants began to speak.

"I know you been getting plenty of time to yourself in there and you're starting to see things differently. You ain't really did no time and now you already sounding like you on some Martin Luther King we shall overcome shit right now. This just me speaking. At first, I was sure we could trust you and everything was solid, but now I'm starting to second guess things. Your name already fucked up in the streets and now I'm not sure what to believe. Why the fuck would we give up the streets when the streets is all some of us have big executive boss. I ain't with this new and improved bull shit you got going on. I'm a street nigga and I don't know what this new shit about but I know one thing, I'm out," Ape Shit A.R. says before hanging up the phone.

Triple J kind of knew A.R. would be against the move but he still allowed him to make his own decision. Luckily the hot head street lieutenant caught Triple J in the transitioning phase because it would have been ugly for him before. Especially with his disrespectful tone.

Being the great leader that he was, Triple J continued the conference call.

"It's unfortunate that we had to lose our brother chapter today," Triple J pauses. "It's something I've come to realize over time that everyone's not going to level up with you in life. A good leader will always give the option of growth to his men. This move comes at a difficult time but my main objective is to simply transfer our skills into the world with other business executives. Before I continue, is there anyone else that declines to be a member of The Executive Homies?" Triple J asks.

After several seconds of silence, Triple J continues the conversation.

"So, now that we're all on the same page, new literature will be passed down in our telegram chat. We'll no longer classify as ANW or use any other street term. From now on we are board members and everything that we do will be voted and vetted on. I have to go, My Executive Homies. The meeting is adjourned," Triple J ends the conference call.

Jew Boy looks at him with a huge smile on his face.

"What you think?" Triple J asks.

"Man, I don't know but this Shit Just Got 2 Real."

18

While lying on his custom comfort Triple J calculated his next moves. Now that there was no more ANW he knew he was in for a big transition. The Executive Homies had to be run. If not, the Feds would surely be on their bumpers hard. Especially while working the stock market.

Man, this case just needs to get over with, he says to himself.

While he's planning his next moves, three deputies approach his cell.

"Johnson! Get dressed, you have an attorney visit," the older male wearing the white shirt says.

Triple J knew he was due for an attorney visit soon, especially after the call he made to Unk.

"Oh shit! It's about that time to hear some good news," Jew Boy says. "I know they about to let you go. You cost too much money to keep in here."

Hell yeah, it's been time to go, Triple J smiles. *But sometimes no news is the best news.*

Getting up and dressing himself, the crime boss moves quicker than he normally would. Doctors had recently given him a walking cane since the new physical therapy update, but also allowed him to keep his chair just in case. Since he was going down stairs, to the attorney booth, he used his chair to be cautious.

Lt. Washington is what the name tag said on the highest-ranking officer. He was present, but stood back as the deputies handcuffed and shackled Triple J.

"Captain James sent me to make sure you were good," Lt. Washington says, breaking the awkward silence.

"Oh yes, tell the Captain everything is fairly midline. Just eager to see what's going to come of all of this."

"You'll be okay. Just make sure you keep the Father, Son and Holy Spirit in your life," Lt. Washington responds.

Triple J paused for a second because he never really believed in Christianity, even after Pop became a pastor.

How can I keep them first when I don't even know them? When I died, I was face to face with my ancestors. I didn't see The Father, The Son or the Holy Spirit. But that's neither here nor there.

"Yes Sir!" Triple J replies.

"And don't forget to read Psalms 91 & 27 every day. It will get you through the hard times. Trust me young man," Lt. Washington says before resting his hands on Triple J's shoulder.

I can't focus on all that right now Unk. I'm fighting for my life and you talking about some lame as Bible verse. Ain't none of that gone stop these white folks from giving my ass the death penalty. I need to hear some real shit not this Bible bull shit but that's neither here nor there either.

The officers safely escorted him down to the second floor where the attorneys' booths are. The entire floor was on lockdown since the case was a high profile. No inmates or staff were allowed to move for safety and preliminary precautions.

Already inside Torris J, Triple J's attorney sat and waited.

"Mr. Johnson! It's good to see you. How you holding up in there?" TJ asks.

"It's been a journey. I've traveled down tougher roads and this is just seasoning for the good things being prepared," Triple J replies.

"Well, it's good to see you're in good spirits, Mr. Johnson. Last week your uncle gave me a call and stopped by my office with a healthy payment. It was enough for us to build a great team of co-counsel in your defense. You know Bruce Arvey, Don Sanders and the best appeals attorney of all time my good friend Bryan Steerler. I'll be leading the defense and they'll work on witnesses and expert testimonies. I had to get all big wheels together for this one since you're that big of a deal in this town. It's some big people that's not very fond of Triple J and want you to rot away."

Triple J knew that to be true. His big question was simply, *Who?*

The Atlanta City was his city. Who other than Triple J was born and raised in the A and represented on the highest level? Nobody!

James Johnson, Jr. provided legal and illegal jobs, opened doors and opportunities for all ATLiens, kept the corporate giants in check all while being a great husband to his wife at the same time.

I am Atlanta City and I'm gone represent my shit. COA, COE City of Atlanta, City over Everything! Anybody coming for the throne know what's going on and should get good and gone.

"I know this is crazy Mr. Johnson and it's really going to

get crazier now. I hate to be the bearer of bad news all the time but yesterday I received an email and certified mail letter from the DA's office with some more disturbing news. Your case has been re-indicted with 28 co-conspirators and 55 counts. This DA is going after everyone and I'm sure they are just doing this to get someone to flip on you," T.J. says.

This definitely was another shocker for Triple J but he was prepared to fight, especially with the legal team he has.

Looking at the new indictment papers, Count number 1 of the 88 page indictment was CONSPIRACY TO VIOLATE THE RACKETEER INFLUENCED AND CORRUPT ORGANIZATIONS ACT.

Damn, we just got hit with the RICO ACT, was all that he could think while shaking his head from left to right. Being the man in his position he knew that he was going down. As he looked down the long list of Co-defendants, all he could do was shake his head. All of his closest associates were listed on the indictment, some names he didn't recognize. Strolling down the list twice already he took a third look to make sure he didn't miss something.

"Is there a page missing or something?" Triple J asked his attorney.

"Umm, No sir. It's all there. The page numbers are actually printed at the bottom right-hand corner."

"Thank you! I thought so." Triple J replies with a hint of anger in his voice.

"Is there something you would like for me to look into?" TJ asks.

"Naw I got it. This is personal. But I do have a question. Why is my name the only one listed twice on the indictment?"

"Umm! One is Jr and the other is…" Torris J began to say before his ears went deaf.

Shit Just Got 2 Real!

$\mathcal{W}$hen it seemed like things couldn't get any worse it did. The state had come crashing down on the entire crime family hard. Triple J had already been indicted on murder charges but the re-indictment was horrific. Fulton's DA's office was going after the entire family, old and new. His mind wandered hard as he questioned his father's reasoning for being on the ANW crime family RICO indictment.

How did I let Pop get caught up in this shit? Triple J asks himself. *There is no way I'm going to let the old man go down. It's just no way,* he continues.

James J, Triple J's father had been out of the game for a while now, leaving everything to his son. Although at one point he led the crime family his days of criminal activity were done for.

In disbelief, Triple J reflected on recent conversations with his pop.

The game been good to me. I know a lot of brothers I went to school with, that never got a chance to see the good life, Pop said reflecting.

The attorneys' visit was done and Triple J knew he had to get back to his cell asap to notify everyone.

"Hey, Lt Washington I really appreciate you taking your time with me, but I need to use the restroom," Triple J says holding up two fingers indicating it was an emergency.

The message was received and Lt Washington and his guys sped him to his cell.

The heat had come down on ANW and Triple J knew the guys were probably oblivious to what was happening. Time was critical right now and it was his responsibility to inform the guys, giving them heads up, before the fugitive squad went to pick people up.

In his cell Jew Boy smiled at the door as the Executive was returning. Stone faced and firm Triple J showed no emotion as the officers pushed him in.

"They got us fucked man. They got us fucked up!" Triple J says banging on his arm chair after the door closes.

"What's going on?" Jew Boy asks.

"It's the bitch ass nigha. The bitch ass nigha man. He was supposed to be my brother," Triple J says with extreme rage in his voice.

Lt. Washington and the other deputies left the range, Triple J pulled his phone from the spot behind the toilet.

As soon as he powered it on, several text alerts began to come through. Without checking them, he already knew what it was. The feds had run down on everybody listed on the indictment. A strong feeling hit him that the news would be airing the arrest, so he immediately went to the local news website and there it was Breaking News.

Breaking News

New this morning, several members of the ANW crime family were arrested after an 88-page RICO indictment was released to the public.

"These gangs make up over 80% of the crime in our city and I refuse to allow this to continue," District Attorney Paul Howie says in a news conference interview. "I was elected to bring forth peace in Atlanta and that's what I'm here to do. As I said during my campaign, I'm here to bring down all involved with gangs, mobs, cliques and crime families whatever, big or small. My office has invested an extensive amount of resources into this investigation, following this particular crime family for several decades. We have witness evidence that local Pastor James Johnson, Sr. once led the organization and used his church as a cover for criminal activity. My team of investigators have years' worth of evidence and for several of the ANW members lengthy prison sentences will be passed down. These menace men will be off of our streets making Atlanta and its metropolitan area safer for our residents and their families. Please note this is just the beginning of our city sweep and message to you gangsters if you're in a gang or associated, your name will be next on our future indictment. I'll see you all on the 6th day of January when James "Triple J" Johnson Jr. will be in court picking a jury. Fulton's DA says before walking away from the podium.*

Triple J closes the browser page and locks his phone screen. Overhearing the news report, Jew Boy knew that things were critical for the ex- crime boss, especially starting trial so soon with this new indictment. Although he didn't see the different video clips of the other ANW members being arrested, he could see the distress in the executives' eyes. Neither of them could understand why things were happening the way they were, for the both of them it was tough.

"It's gone work out for the good, Big Executive," Jew Boy says. "I can feel it."

Triple J wanted to believe what he was saying had some truth in it, especially since his grandfather told him that once before, but shit just keeps getting real.

When is it going to make sense? He asked himself while reflecting over his life.

Many times, the ex-crime boss would play a game of chess in his brain. First there were pawns then the who, what, when, where and why? Reflecting on how his old man left him the family business, blemish free, Triple J refused to allow him to go down with them. Some pieces had to be moved and some pawns had to be sacrificed. The streets had a way of making you feel as though you were family but in all actuality, there was no such thing. Everybody was for self, especially now these felony charges were being passed out.

No one is to be trusted, Triple J reminds himself. *"Not even the most trusted."*

A sour taste filled his mouth and as he rushes towards the toilet his right leg gives and he barf all over the front of the young Jew Boy shirt who tries to catch him.

"Blaargh!"

"Damn, this shit stank like hot cheese and spoiled milk," Jew Boy says while struggling to lift the Executive Homeboy.

"My fault! You know I definitely didn't mean to get you like that." Triple J says expressing his grief but to him that was only a sign.

"You good Big Exec! I'm glad I was here to have your back," Jew Boy says as he pulls the ill ridden shirt over his head.

"I know you do but I need you to get me from outside the fort. A lot is going on right now," Triple J tells him without looking him in the eyes.

Jew Boy was good company but too much has happened and Triple J needed to be alone. Struggling to hide the emotional disparity on his face, sadness could still be felt as the young guy packed his property. As the floor officer did his security rounds, Jew Boy stopped him.

"Hey I need you to call the Sergeant or Lieutenant, I'm leaving this room," he said.

The officer knew he shared the space with, so he immediately opened the door and allowed the young guy to remove his property, without a question.

"Stay up Young Exec," Triple J says as he's leaving out.

"Man, Fuck You!" Jew Boy replies in raging anger.

Shit Just Got 2 Real.

20

*T*wo days after the re-indictment, Triple J was finally headed back into court.

"God I'll be glad when this is over," he says to himself.

His unfortunate injury, several months ago, pushed the case back and this new indictment really caused heavy anxiety. Sitting in a freezing cold holding cell, his legs shake rapidly as he waits for arraignment. Several tactical dressed officers stand outside his cell waiting for the court proceedings to begin.

"Mr. Johnson you alright in there," one of the deputies asked.

"Yes! It's just a little cold and I'm ready to get this over," Triple J replies.

"Alright I'm gone check and see how much time we got to wait, but in the meantime, how do you feel about us putting one other person in there with you?" The deputy asks.

"It's cool, hopefully the room will then warm up."

Two cells down, an older gentleman sat quietly in leg irons and in handcuffs. At the time the deputies had so many 'keep separates', they didn't know who was who and who couldn't be in the same cell. Having the older gentleman change cells was something neither of them was prepared for.

Walking through the cell door with his Bible in hand, a smile spreads across the face of the incarcerated pastor.

"Baba!" Triple J screams as he stands up from his wheelchair for his old man.

Neither of them cared to see each other in this way, but seeing each other was most important.

"How you holding up?" Pastor Johnson asks his son.

"I can walk again. Shit had got real for me," Triple J replies.

"You're a Johnson. Those things are going to happen, you just have to keep your head up and keep moving."

"I know Baba. I know. I just feel really bad," Triple J says, holding his head down in distress.

"Pick your head up," he says, clenching his teeth.

"You're a Johnson, don't ever let them see you down," Pastor Johnson continues to motivate his son.

"I know Baba, I'm just concerned about you going to prison."

"Concerned! I see you done forgot who made you Triple J," Pastor Johnson says, being sarcastic. "I'm a Johnson , you should never be concerned about me. If anything, you should be concerned about the prison they send me to. I'm the ordained pastor and they got prison ministry. I'm gone save more souls from the pits of hell, than the law can imagine," he continues before winking his eyes.

Triple J laughs before a long exhale.

"Whoo! I feel so much better. This has been stressful

Baba, a lot of stress has been on me with this death penalty, hanging over my head," Triple J tells his father.

"Son," Pastor Johnson says, taking a pause, "We've done what we've done and excelled further than what they could imagine. Always remember this, Earth is like a marketplace and Heaven is our home. Don't ever get comfortable here. These times are trying times and we all have to be tried like Job. The devil tried Job and took everything from the man, even his family. When the smoke cleared and everything settled God blessed him with double of everything. There's a home in Heaven, God's prepared for us. I promise it's way more riches there than earth could ever imagine."

Triple J stared at his father and smiled as tears began to fill his eyes. Pastor Johnson being the senior of the two always directed his junior well. The deputies may have mistakenly or purposely placed them together and Triple J really appreciated them. The conversation with his pop was very much needed.

Breaking up their conversation, the tactical dressed deputy Sergeant tapped on the glass.

"Johnson, they're ready for you in court," he says.

"Which one?" They ask together.

"James Johnson," he answers.

"Which one," they ask a second time.

The Sargent looks at the two with confusion all over his face, as he realizes they're father and son.

"Well, I'll be damn," he says. "I gotta go back in there and see which one of y'all they want, junior or senior."

They both laugh at the confused facial expression on the Sargent's face, as he leaves shaking his head.

"Okay! Let's try this again. James Johnson, Jr they're ready for you in court."

Triple J stands again and grabs his father's hand in the handcuffs. Slightly bowing his head, he then receives a kiss from his father on his forehead.

"We gone be alright, son. They may control where your body goes but you control the thoughts in your mind. Stay focused and keep your head up son," Pastor Johnson says before his son sits back in his chair and the deputies roll him out.

As Triple J rolled down the hallway to the courtroom, he was very much so relieved to know that his father would be okay incarcerated.

We're Johnson's and Johnson's can't be broken, he reminds himself as he's wheeled into the courtroom.

Despite the jam-packed courtroom, the first thing that he saw was the black eye of the news camera lenses facing him.

Here we go again, Triple J says to himself.

"How are you holding up?" Torris J asks knowing his client was struggling.

"I just seen pops in the back, they had us in the cell together," he whispers in his attorney's ear.

"How's he holding up?"

"He's good. But I need you to get him out of here though. This ain't no place for the old man." Triple J whispers with emphasis in his voice.

"Let me make some calls, I'll do my best," Torris J assures.

The prosecutor began to speak and although Triple J's life was on the line the whole hearing was simply a show to him.

"Your honor this RICO case and the persons involved are very dangerous especially the shot caller, James "Triple J" Johnson, Jr. He has a special troop of ANW crime family members that he directly communicates and financially funds to commit heinous crimes. These crimes include extortion, assaults, robberies and murders. Although he's not actually hands-on with these crimes, he's even worse than the ones committing them because he's the one sending them," the Assistant District Attorney says.

Triple J keeps a stone face while the presentation is going on. After several minutes of listening to the DA's address to the court, he finally shuts out the negativity.

This is all a stage play to these folks that involves my life. I refuse to keep stressing this shit. They gone do what they wanna do. Why am I even tripping on this shit. Even Baba told me it's going to look rough in the beginning but everything is going to work out for me in the end, he reminds himself. *I'm gone be alright.*

Shit Just Got 2 Real.

$\mathcal{J}$t was one of the greatest feelings in the world, to finally have the mental and emotional freedom, even with his case still pending. It didn't matter what jail or cell they placed the ex-crime boss in, the clock didn't stop just because the lock had locked. Triple J had not one worry in the world and his glow could be seen by everyone he encountered. When the doors popped for them to have their hour out, he was one of the first out of his cell.

"You looking good Nephew, I can see you in the dark and the light," Mr. Robinson, the eldest inmate in the medical unit says.

Mr. Robinson was the smoothest seventy-year-old Triple J has ever met. His jailhouse moniker was Civil Rights, a name he gained after dropping so many old skool jewels on the young fools. He didn't talk to many but if he saw something in you, then you were in for a treat. Rumor has it he was originally from Chicago, but no one actually knew. Triple J asked him once and all he could do was chuckle at the old man's response.

"Can't no one town hold me, Baby Boy!" He squinted his eyes and said in a very serious tone. "You know, one time this local joker corral thought they had a going on nephew and tried to recruit me to join them. Before they could get their gang of five roommates together to initiate me, I had already crossed two continents, seven counties, and eleven seas," he says, making everyone in the room laugh. "I'm an international player, Baby Boy. Can't no one town hold me."

During their recreation time, the two of them talked as they walked laps around the dorm. Since the jail's medical doctors cleared him of all restrictions, Triple J utilized most of that free time for physical fitness.

At seventy, Mr. Robinson was no workout slouch either. Whatever Triple J did he did too, push-ups, sit-ups, crunches and squats. The usual workout was carried out with 10 sets with 25 reps equaling 250 total.

"You looking good Baby Boy," Mr. Robinson said, complementing Triple J's physique.

The physical therapy and cell workouts had him feeling and looking like his old self times five.

"I preshate ya, Unk," he says looking down at his comeback core. "Nothing can stop me now."

"Nothing could stop you before Baby Boy. The only thing that's changed is your price. Whatever you did it for before, is now times ten because the price of a player dun went up." Mr. Robinson says winking his eye with a slight head tilt at Triple J.

"I like that. The price of a player dun went up," Triple J repeats.

"Seriously! You paid the price to get where you at, now they got to pay that price ten times over. You've planted your seeds and now all you got to do is keep doing what you're doing for your harvest."

Everything Mr. Robinson said was true, Triple J put in the work and it was definitely his harvest season. After they finished their work out and took showers, it was time for lockdown. Before the cells closed, Mr. Robinson left him with a reminder.

"The price of a player just went up," he says before their cell doors close.

That's right the price of a player just went up.

Word traveled through Inmate.com that Triple J was back on his feet. A few people wanted to see him down, but still so many wanted to see his recovery. When one particular individual heard he was back walking she had to see for herself.

"Mr. Johnson!" She sings in her beautiful voice. "I need you to get dressed and come with me."

Triple J looks up and sees his jailhouse bae, Lieutenant Rogers. She's standing in front of his cell window with a huge smile stretching the skin across her face. Her bulletproof vest could be seen under her polo style uniform shirt and plump rump under her service belt. Lieutenant Rodgers had the body of a goddess and there was not a single pair of pants that could hide her curves. Everybody inside and out of the jail liked looking at her backside, especially the inmates. Most of the inmates were intimidated and afraid of her and her assets, all but Triple J. She was crazy over him and that's how he liked it.

He quickly gets dressed and once he's ready she holds up a large ring of keys, searching through them for the one to his cell. Once opening the cell door, she places a set of purple and platinum handcuffs on him, restraining his hands in the front.

"They not too tight right?" She asks with genuine concern.

"Naw they good," he replies.

Since his first day of incarceration, Triple J's name has been one of the most notorious names ringing around Fulton Jail. Regularly mentioned in the administrative halls, James Johnson Jr, was the highest of high-profile detainees ever housed inside Fulton Jail. When Lt. Rodgers walked him onto the hallway one of the tops turned into a Stan, Triple J's number one fan, when he saw him.

"Mr. Johnson what's going on it's good to see you walking again," he says like he's one of The Executive Homies.

Triple J was aware that he was a white shirt, which meant he was high ranking. On his shirt collar silver oak leaf insignia are worn, and at the time Triple J was unaware of what they represented. All until he sees the name stitched, opposite of his sheriff's badge, Lt Col. Perry.

Lt Col. Perry was a 26-year veteran with the Sheriff's Department and everyone loved him. His jailhouse moniker was Colonel Cooly, a name given by the inmates for his humble and hip swagger. Lt Col. Perry was one of the most admired administrators especially with the staff because he helped day to day operations flow smoothly.

"Colonel Cooly!" Triple J says calling him by his moniker.

"Yes, that's what they call me," Lt Col. Perry replies with a chuckle and smile.

"It's nice to finally meet you, I heard so much about you sir," Triple J says, patronizing the man.

"Hopefully all good things," he replies again with a laugh.

"If it wasn't, you would know. When you're not around, I'll protect ya name, wouldn't let 'em talk about ya," Triple J says singing the late Mo3's popular song.

They all laugh before Triple J and Lt. Rodgers continue to her office. She removes his hand restraints and directs him to the chair in front of her desk.

"Have a seat," she says before sitting behind her desk. "I brought you down here today because I need your help. This new indictment has my classification department in shambles and we don't know what to do. The higher ups wanna move y'all into a dormitory together and I thought it would be best to talk with you first before we made that move."

"I'm not opposed to that. What's this deal with this protective status shit y'all was talking about earlier?" Triple J asks.

Lt Col. Perry said, "If you're ready to return to General Population, then we will let you go. That's why we're having this talk today."

Triple J was definitely ready to get back to General Population. Nothing would stop him from getting with his Exec's. This was the perfect move for them to get everything established.

"Hell yeah, I wanna get back to population. Triple J says.

"Alright we'll make the move today," Lieutenant Rogers says.

"One last thing."

"What's that?" She asks.

"Put me and my daddy in the same room," he tells her.

"Okay! I can do that," she tells him.

Moving all of his guys together was more than money can buy. A dormitory full of The Executive Homies, was a true blessing and they couldn't do anything less than level up. Legally!

Shit Just Got 2 Real.

22

Clearing an entire dormitory out, for The Executive Homies, was a chaotic transition. None of the former ANW members knew what was taking place and even bucked forcing the floor officers to call the emergency response team for help.

"This some bullshit. Y'all keep moving a nigga around like cattle," one of Triple J's close homies complained.

"It's not us. The big dogs made this call," one of the green team members replied while restoring order.

To move a total of 54 inmates it took exactly five hours and four two minutes. They had one last move before they could get off.

"Johnson let's do it," Sargent Riley says when he approaches Triple J's cell.

"I'm ready!" He replies with a quickness property packed at the cell door.

A sense of nervousness crossed over his mind as he marched down the medical corridor. Offices on both sides were filled with medical staff all surprised when they saw the famous Triple J. Most of the ladies heard about him but none of them actually saw him in person.

"You alright Johnson?" Sargent Riley asked.

"Yeah, I'm good just preparing myself for what's to come," Triple J replies.

"You good they made a whole ANW dorm for y'all," Sarge replies.

"That's alright but it's still a lot to come with that. I gotta make sure all of these niggas eat, everybody looking for me to give them a hand out," Triple J replies.

"Don't look at it like that," Sargent Riley replies. "Look at it as God's way of challenging you to be one of the great leaders in history. Did you know Malcom X, MLK and Nelson Mandela all did time? Two of them have Nobel Peace Prizes, one became the President. You think their people wasn't in need of aid? That's what they fought for the people in need, civil rights and apartheid. They had folks fighting for food, desegregation of the buses, the simple rights to being human. You should use this time like "Tookie" Williams did and become a civil leader, leading your guys to freedom. I can see it now, Triple J the Great!" Sargent Riley says in a chant.

The shit he was saying had got 2 real and Triple J agreed, he was right. He was responsible for leading his guys to freedom, breaking the chains that's kept them in mental slavery for so long.

The ride up the elevator was silent and Triple J knew it was time for him to officially stamp all of his homies to The Executive Homies. As Sargent Riley pushed the cart towards 7 North, the opposite side of where he was before, a nervous feeling came across him.

"Whew!" Triple J exhaled hard.

Sargent Riley looked at him and smiled.

"You're good, just remember what I said," he assured him. "Now, I'm looking for you to become something big when you get out of here. Don't disappoint me."

"I promise you I won't," Triple J replied.

"Tower! Open 7 North," Sargent Riley says into the intercom.

When the 900 doors began to slide, excitement raced through Triple J's veins like a fighter entering the ring. Mark Morrison's *Return of the Mack* played in his head giving him that winner's energy as he crossed over the 7 North threshold.

Sargent Riley placed Triple J's 3 card, identification paper, in the shoot for the tower to pull it up.

"Is that Johnson," the female officer in the tower asks.

"Yes, he's coming from MOU and he needs a mattress," Sargent Riley says.

"We had the orderly put one in his cell. He's going to cell 508," she says.

"Alright Johnson, I've got to go. Keep your head up and stay focused. This too shall pass," Sarge says.

Triple J grabs his property from the rolling cart and walks into the 500 dormitories. As his cell door opens the entire dorm erupts into loud cheers.

"Big Homie," he heard a few of them scream, excited to see their leader.

As he walked in, he envisioned himself as an Executive taking stage in front of a crowd of young and hungry entrepreneurs. His heart was filled with Joy as he locked eyes with his dad and biggest supporter, James Jay.

The time is now, he says to himself.

Triple J sets his property down on the floor before

walking up the chair to stand on the tabletop. Sargent Riley mentioned that it was past time for him to go off and when Triple J began to address the dorm, he was patient.

"Greetings Great Men, for those of you that don't know there is no more ANW. We're no longer identifying ourselves as animals, mobsters, criminals, gangsters or illegals. We are all businessmen and from now on, we address ourselves as one thing and one thing only Executive's. I'm your Executive Homeboy and we all are The Executive Homies. Tonight, I would like for you all to draw up your own business plan. I want you to write down everything that you're going to need with the business starting with the legal documents to the supplies, location and everything else needed to run a business. We all have a 50k start up budget. I wanna see what you got in the morning. My Executive I'm no different from yours. The first step to success is application. Tonight's exercise is our application to a successful future in business. I got Sarge waiting for me to go inside but before I do I wanna say this. This is our time to seek knowledge and apply the knowledge we receive to our everyday lives. The unimaginable is happening for us and my executives. I love you," Triple J says before receiving a hand from his Pops off the table.

From behind the cell doors loud claps could be heard way out into the hallway of 7 north.

"You did a good job son," James J says, hugging his son.

As soon as they enter their cell, the tower officer closes the cell door behind them.

Triple J sees his father has his bunk made up on the top.

"You get the bottom bed Pop," Triple J says.

"Naw! I'm gone be just fine up here," he says, tapping the top bunk twice.

"If that's what you say," Triple J says before making up his bunk.

"I'm glad to see you in good health, son. They had me afraid when they told me you were in a coma," James Jay says.

"Man, I can only imagine how that was on you," he says with a sigh.

"Son, have a seat," James Jay says, grabbing his son's hand stopping him from making up his bunk.

They both lock eyes with each other before James Jay sits his son on the bunk.

"While you were in the coma, I stayed down at the hospital talking to doctors and nurses praying for you son. I told God before he takes my son, he can have my life. I started experiencing a severe pain in my lower back and collapsed to the floor. Doctors rushed me to the ER and after several tests were run, they found I have Stage 4 kidney cancer," his father said.

It was like a wrecking ball was hitting him in the chest and immediately all Triple J could do now was sigh.

Shit Just Got 2 Real.

23

*T*he next morning, at 7am prompt, the cell doors throughout the 500 dormitory began to open. Triple J was slow to get up but knew he had to shake it for the 7:00am count. Last night was tough on him getting the news about his father having Stage 4 Kidney cancer. Quietly he cried himself to sleep, after finding out his Pops chances of survival were very low.

I don't need this right now, Triple J thought as he was getting out of the bed.

All his life all he had was his pops and the streets. The streets were full of fake love but that real genuine love came from Pop Johnson. None of the other Executives knew what was going on so it was important for him to keep his composure, despite everything else he was going through.

Standing tall at his cell door for count, James Jay held his head high with a huge smile on his face. Although he was dying inside there was nothing better than the present.

"I see you're having a good morning," Sargent Kelly says as she flips through the book of 3 cards.

"It's always a blessing to be in the land of the living," Pop Johnson replies.

Triple J just nodded his head when she got to him, not really in the mood to talk.

After count, Sargent Kelly addresses the dorm.

"Alright guys, I'm expecting good things out of y'all while you're up here. The orderly is going to get y'all some cleaning supplies to clean your cells. Then I need one of you to stay out after lockdown to clean the dorm for me. If you need anything, hit the intercom. I'm going to be in the tower. Okay!" Sargent Kelly says.

"Yes ma'am," several of the guys in the dorm said.

As soon as she left and the 500 doors began to close, most of the dorm headed down to Triple J's cell.

"I can't call you Big Ape no more, so what's up Big Executive," his executive homie formerly known as Ape Shit Flames says.

"My Brother," Triple J says, hugging his homie.

"I miss you my nigga," Flames says.

"I miss you too," Triple J replies.

The last time they saw each other they were roommates and Triple J had left for an attorney visit. Inmate.com has so much to say about what happened but no one actually knew the facts. One thing Flames did know to be true, was that Triple J was no informant. After the big Rico indictment, there was one man missing that was supposed to be there. Everybody knew that he started the rumor and since his name was the only one missing in the case he had to be cooperating.

"So, what's up with this Executive homies shit you got going on. Who you supposed to be, Russ Simone or some shit now?" Flames asks, gaining laughter from the other guys in the dorm.

"No but if that's what you wanna be, I can help you mirror his position," Triple J replies to his sarcasm.

"Hell naw that's you, The Executive Homeboy," Flames replies. "I'm a thug I go Ape shit," Flames replies getting the other guys to agree with him.

"Understandable, for most of us that's what we're taught. So, we assume that's all we know how to do," Triple J says looking into the eyes of the crowd of guys before him. "We assume we have to obtain four-year bachelor's degrees in business management to own a business. We assume it takes a bunch of startup money and we can't put it in our names. Did you know because we're felons we're at an advantage? It's actually government business grants and loans out there for minority males and felons. All we need is the proper documentation to get it," Triple J says getting their attention. "I asked y'all last night to draw up a business plan. Flames I know you are good at drawing but look beyond the art. Look at the art business, art galleries, art dealers. It's the same thing we been doing, just a different product. Now we sell art instead of phones, cigarettes and weed."

"That's right," Flames agreed, shaking his head up and down with the other guys.

"It's just like when we buy hellcats and scat packs, the dealer gives us pink slips showing ownership. To transfer ownership, we sign a Bill of Sale, from Seller to Buyer. It's all the same shit. Only difference is we're on the Dealers end of the table now. The man that makes the most money is the man that does the least work. The Executive!" Triple J says. "Starting a business and allowing other people to work puts you in position to settle down and travel with your family.

That's when you become the socket and they become the Plug! Remember you are the one with the work."

"Hell yeah, Hell yeah!" Several of them say in unison.

"I know y'all enjoy going Ape shit, I once did. But I promise it's a whole different feeling when you're flying private 35,000 feet in the air with a bad bitch riding your lap," Triple J says, making them smile. "That's when you wanna leave all the bull shit alone just so you don't lose the wonderful feeling," Triple J continues.

"So how do we get there," The Executive Mazi asks?

"That's a good question Mazi. It's definitely a process to get there because nothing comes overnight. In business you have to be patient, committed and persistent. I gave y'all a business plan assignment to do last night and today I'm going to look over what you got. I'm going to help you tweak them, have some lawyers come and help with the Secretary of State paperwork and of the five I like most I'm going to donate 50k a piece for the start up. With the other companies we're going to apply for government grants and funding. One thing I can say is that we're all going to have our own legal business before we leave here," Triple J assures them.

Not everyone was excited about the new move and Triple J understood that.

"All that executive shit sound good and all, but what we gone do about this RICO case?" One of the homies asks.

"We fight!" Triple J answers in a stern and serious tone. "We've been physical warriors all of our lives naturally. This is a different type of fight and that's why I want you to use your brains and get out of that street bull shit mindset. We dealing with educated mother fuckers now that wanna take our lives. We're dealing with racist mother fuckers now that don't wanna see us father our kids. They don't care about nothing but the U.S. Dollar. I'm trying to put all of us in position to have a fighting chance. Some of us will fall and some will walk free. That's what happens in war. For those of us that fall we still have something to fall back on and with that U.S. Dollar we can hire the best appeal attorney to get the fuck out of this shit," Triple J says sounding like a sports coach in the huddle. He pauses for a second and tears begin to form in his eyes. "Before I went into the coma my lawyer came to see me. The State is trying to give me the death penalty which means I'm probably going to be put to rest by lethal injection," he continues with tears falling from his eyes. "I understand the consequences. I started this shit and I know what I was doing. I'm good. I've lived a life many couldn't even imagine. This is not the end for me, this is not the end of us. That Ape spirit must live for generations to come and the only way we leave generational wealth to our kids is by arranging for our deaths today," he finishes.

Triple J looked at his father who continued to hold his head tall despite the painful cancer cells eating at his body. James Jay nods his head at his son, signaling to him to stay strong despite the reality. The entire room could feel the pain in his voice as they thought about the depressing reality they were facing. Neither of them wanted to be a casualty of war, but for some the rest of their life would be incarceration. The thought alone was enough to make a grown man cry.

Shit Just Got 2 Real.

24

*D*epression wanted to get the best of Triple J, but Pop Johnson wasn't allowing it. He began to prepare them both mentally, physically and spiritually, for the difficult times ahead. Sharing a cell with his son was an immeasurable blessing and they took full advantage of it. Pop Johnson knew there were a few lessons he needed to pass on to his son and the best way would be over a game of chest.

Seated on the bottom bunk, with the chess board between them, Pop Johnson begins his schooling.

"Chess is the game of life," he says, as they're setting the board piece. "This is a thinking man's game and once you master this, you'll maneuver through life 'piece fully,'" he says metaphorically.

"Oh, is that right old school?" Triple J asks with a chuckle.

"Old School!" Pop Johnson says surprised. "I like that. So, you're the young school right. You're a part of this new group that's been spoiled your whole life and now you think you know everything. Cheers to a good whipping," Pop Johnson says, holding up his coffee cup comically.

"To the best man," Triple J responds respectfully to his dad.

The old man didn't come to play opening with an aggressive white move, Triple J takes mental notes of it. He sees his attempt at a Danish Gambit, but instead of taking the pawn on his second move, he brings out his knight to defend the center of the board. Pop sits up on the bed adjusting his view of the board and Triple J knew then that he had his attention.

Although they were playing against each other, Triple J still maintained a lot of respect for his father. On their first game he could have easily beat the old man, but instead of abusing the elderly he closed out the game in a stalemate. After pulling out a few tricks from under his sleeves he beats the old man viciously the next two games.

"That's called the underlay for the overlay," Triple J says, talking a little smack after his two victories.

Pop Johnson respected his son's 2-0 lead, congratulating him after the small win.

"You play good Baby Boy, beating up on the old man with all them tricky tricks. It's the best out of five, right?" Pop Johnson asks.

"I thought it was best two out of three, but if you want the best out of five it's cool with me," Triple J answers humbly.

The next three games, Pop Johnson beat the soul out his son. He made The Executive Homie look like he was just an entry level sales man, beating him like a thief that just got caught stealing. Pop Johnson set up moves that were so unorthodox, before Triple J could see what was happening it was already mate.

"You play a sucker to catch a sucker. Always remember that son," Pop Johnson says, talking his smack now.

"You for damn sure, played me like a sucker," Triple J says laughing at his failure.

"I didn't play you, I let you play yourself. You're the one that underestimated your opponent. I had already won when you called me old school. All I did was play the old school game, play a sucker to catch a sucker," Pop Johnson says shaking his son's hand. "You were victorious the first two games and then you relaxed. I capitalized. You prepared your mind to play best two out of three, so on the third game you was already psychologically exhausted. I saw that and challenged you to best out of five, leaving you with one more game to take the win. You gave up on yourself son," Pop Johnson says looking his son in the eyes. "Always remember this one thing, a fight never starts until it's over. Channel your strength levels to 10 percent physical and 90 percent mental. Wish for the best but prepare for the worst. No matter the score, you always fight the good fight. If you lose the battle keep fighting until you win the war," Pop Johnson says to his son.

Soaking up the free game, Triple J makes sure to store his father's teachings in his heart. Everyone knew James Jay was the greatest in all that he did, certified, stamped, filed and sealed as the Greatest of All Times.

"The last thing I want you to always remember son, before you talk your little shit, I'm the block, you're just a chip off the block." Pop Johnson says laughing.

"You're definitely right about that," Triple J says acknowledging his father's victory.

Pop Johnson clears the pieces from the board and dumps them in the small carry bag he stores them in. Leaving his son with time to process his life lesson, he jumps to the top bunk.

Laying back on the bunk he reflects over the life lessons his father has taught him.

You play a sucker to catch a sucker, he remembers most because that's exactly how he feels. *Never underestimate your opponent. The fight is 90 percent mental, 10 percent physical. Always fight the good fight.*

Triple J knew he needed to be prepared after all of the bad stories he's heard about prison. Doing the time wasn't his worry the unsafe conditions were though; wars, fighting and stabbing. Triple J recognized that he played relax on the game board against his Pops and learned a very valuable lesson, never underestimate your opponent.

After about a 45 minute meditation moment, he digs his phone from the hole in his mattress. Powering up, he sees several missed call alerts cover the screen.

He made it, Triple J says when he sees the missed calls are from his satellite phone.

"Bonk, bonk," DonJuan says, making a car horn sound when he answers.

"Okay Cool!" Triple J replies in his fly guy tone.

The car horn, "Bonk, Bonk," sound was their code for arriving. In this case, DonJuan was letting Triple J know that he had made it back to Atlanta.

"You didn't tell me the old man was your Uncle," DonJuan says.

"Yes! He's my great uncle," Triple J replies with a smile.

DonJuan knew he couldn't mention his Uncle's name over the phone; it would set off all kinds of national security alerts so he just referred to him as Uncle.

"He made me hurry back with this message. He said 'You're covered on the inside, just keep fighting.'"

Triple J then knew the outcome of his case was going to be devastating based on the response that his great uncle sent back

"Thank you Brother! I owe you for this," Triple J replies genuinely.

"Naw, I actually owe you." DonJuan says, causing confusion in the conversation.

Triple J couldn't think of how DonJuan owed him, when this was the reply to a favor. The call was cut short and Triple J lays back on his bunk.

Pop Johnson overhears the phone call from the top bunk and foresees the future.

"You just made the worst move ever in life son," Pop Johnson says. "Your uncle's henchman just got out and now he needs somebody on the inside he can trust. He would have helped you but why would he do that when he needs someone to distribute weight for him. I respect your plans for change with, The Executive Homies and all but you're not going to be able to get out the game until he feels you're at retirement age," his father tells him.

Triple J shakes his head from left to right because he knew his pops was telling the truth.

Shit Just Got 2 Real

25

*E*arly the next morning, Triple J planned to look over everyone's business plan but that idea quickly changed. Matching in a 2x2 formation, a group of forty plus officers flood into the dormitory dressed in all black tactical gear. Stomping their boots, every step of the way, they made enough noise that they were heard on the lower floors. As they march in the dormitory, they're singing military cadences at the top of the lungs.

"Who rock, who rock this house?" the point man asks the group. "We rock, we rock this house," the group responds their voices echoing off the walls.

Triple J watches from his cell window as they march in. He sees two of them carrying individual clear shields with corrections painted across the front in chipped black lettering.

Damn, these folks on the bull shit, he thinks as he watches them march in.

The commander gives them a voice command and they all stop on the same step, clapping their boots together, creating a loud boom. Continuing to look out of his window Triple J sees the group splitting up. One group marching to the top range, while the second stayed down.

Who in the hell is these folks? He asks himself as a long line filed in front of their cells.

All you could see is eyes above there black mask and under there black brimmed hats. Upside down triangles insignia worn on their shirt sleeves had special operations in gold lettering.

"This got to be the Feds," Triple J says to his father that stood beside him also peeking through the window.

"I don't know son. Whoever they are they're serious," he replies.

An officer in front of their cell began to yell at the window.

"T-Shirts, Boxers, Shower shoes, that's it," he says twice.

The cell doors began to open while Pops and Triple J are removing their jail bottoms. The special operations officer looks at them and begins to yell again.

"I said, T-shirts, boxers and shower shoes. Why do y'all motherfuckers still have socks?" He asks angrily.

Triple J looks the officers' eye to eye with a death stare. Ever since the Sargent snuffed him, while he was on the hospital stretcher, he's had vengeance on his mind. His father sees his temper flaring and grabs his shoulder to calm him.

"Just take off your socks," he says before bending down to remove his socks.

"You better listen to the old man. Cause this ain't what you want," the officer says.

Triple J smiles when the officer calls his Pops an old man.

You play a sucker, to catch a sucker. He's reminded.

Going with the flow of the shakedown, Triple J strips down into his birthday suit, passing his clothes off to the officer. He quickly gets dressed after the officer searches his property.

"Walk out backwards with your hands behind your back," The officer says.

Triple J did as he was told, back stepping out of his cell with his hands behind him.

"Okay now step to your left and put your head on the door," the officer continues to instruct him.

Triple J just steps to the side and stares at the door. Quickly several of the special operations officers pile up behind him.

"I ain't no regular CO I'll beat you ass," he says to Triple J. "Now put your fucking head on that door before I smash your shit in the door," he continues.

Triple J slightly looks at him and sees the gang of officers ready to attack him.

They must not know who the fuck I am, he thinks for a second. *It ain't worth it*, he reminds himself before putting his head on the door.

"Don't say nothing else to him. Just let that head come off that door, so I can blast his ass," a female's voice says behind him.

Triple J ignores them both while still keeping his head on the door. He knew that they were just looking for someone to jump on and he refused to be a victim. Pops goes through the motions next before he lays his head on the door next to his son.

"Let them have it," Pop Johnson tells his son.

Triple J nods his head right before he's attacked from the back.

He's kicked into the door before two tactical officers grab him and slams him to the floor.

"Didn't I tell you that you had one last chance," the male officer says as he pushes Triple J's neck into the floor.

"He didn't say anything I did," his pop says.

The officer didn't want to hear what Pops had to say. He had a target on Triple J.

"Get yo hands off me bitch," Triple J spat at him in anger.

The tactical officers had no idea who he was roughing up but quickly learned. As soon as the other guys looked and seen what was happening all chaos broke loose.

"Get yo hands off him," Flames says bucking on the three officers around him.

One of the female officers shot pepper balls at him but Flames continued to buck.

"Fuck wrong with y'all," another one of his homies says stepping towards the tactical officers.

Captain James hears the chaos from the hallway and quickly steps into the dormitory to see what's going on. He sees the guy they have wrestling on the floor is in front of Triple J's cell he immediately rushes in.

"Hey! Hey! Hey!" He screams while quickly moving towards them. "Hold up, hold up, hold the fuck up," he continues yelling over the chaotic crowd. "Get him the fuck off that damn floor right now motherfucker," he orders them.

"One, Two, Three," the two officers say together before picking him up.

Triple J immediately turns and spits into the face of the officer to his right.

"Hey, Hey, Hey let me get him," Captain James says intervening before shit got even more out of control.

"Calm down Johnson. Calm the fuck down." He continues to yell.

Triple J knew Captain James was his people and wasn't there to hurt him so he cooperated with his orders.

Both Triple J and Flames are escorted into the hallway in plastic handcuffs. Flames had been hit with pepper balls so officers took him directly to medical while Triple J was escorted into the 700 zone. There, several deputies were gathered together with State Investigators and other agency officials. Captain James sat Triple J in a chair on the far end of the room.

This some bullshit, Triple J thinks as he watches all of the police congregate.

Although he was angry and upset, he quickly calmed himself after thinking about the potential of losing the cell with his pops. Triple J knew his dad could handle himself in jail, he is slicker than the slickest slickster but it wasn't worth losing that father son time, especially in his condition.

Triple J patiently waits for Captain James to return as he begins to think.

This is crazy how they move all of our guys in the same dorm together then come in with this big shake down. Good thing we put all of the phones up last night.

Promising to never go out bad like he did the last time with his phone in his cell, Triple J had one of his homies that remodels homes, create them a professional hiding spot. In the shower he carved out two tiles and built a pocket in the wall using paper-mâché. It wasn't the biggest hiding place just large enough for them to hide four thin phones. Only three people knew where the spot was so the chances of it getting busted was slim. Every night at exactly 9:30 they had to be ready for put up. The night orderly would pick them up while he swept the dorm with a dust mop. To the officers in the tower, everything looked normal because he worked the entire time. While cleaning the showers, he would dig out the two tiles and put the phones up sealing the tiles with tooth paste. That one spot was good for them all because if ever got busted, no one could be charged. The shower was labeled as a common area, something everyone used.

As he sat there and waited Triple J's thoughts continued to run wild.

This RICO shit don't seem right. Why would they put all of us together and then come shakedown with this much force? What if it was in their plan to pull me out and bring me around all these detective motherfuckers so my people could start speculating again about me cooperating. This shit is not the move, Triple J thinks for a second.

"A man this shit is tight on my wrist," he says getting their attention from the corner of the room.

"You'll be alright. They almost done anyways," the Caucasian male detective says waving Triple J off.

I been in here too long. This shit don't look right, he thinks.

"A MAN! This shit to tight on my wrist," he then yells.

"And I said you'll be alright," the detective replies. "A Captain, this man you brought in here is complaining about the cuffs. Come check on him before I go back to how I use to be," the detective continues.

Captain James walks into 700 from the hallway and checks on Triple J.

"What's going on you good?" He asks.

"Naw this shit cutting my wrist," Triple J replies.

He pulls a pocket knife from his right cargo pocket and gets ready to cut them but can't.

"Oh, shit these really are tight," Captain James says unable to slide his knife in. "Okay! I need you to work with me now. This might hurt but I gotta get it."

Damn I hope this Nigga don't cut me, Triple J thinks.

"Okay on three," Captain James says.

Sliding his knife quickly between the plastic cuffs and Triple J's hands, he cuts them before the count even begins.

"I told you on three," Captain James says with a chuckle after freeing his hands. "You good now?"

"Yeah I'm good. Ya folks was just tripping," Triple J says.

"You gotta let them do their job get in and out of here," Captain James says.

Slamming me to the floor for doing everything they said is not there fucking job. That's an abuse of power. But it don't mean shit! I'm just an inmate, Triple J thinks.

Back in the dormitory, Triple J sees all of his homies lined up in formations with their hands behind their backs. Everyone is facing the wall in T-shirts, boxers and showers shoes.

Triple J closes his eyes at the humiliating sight, before he too stands in formation with them.

An older black woman dressed in the same tactical uniform as the people that slashed him earlier approaches.

"Young man, are you alright," she asks in the softest motherly tone.

Triple J doesn't respond, staring one thousand miles into the head of the person in front him like a U.S. Marine.

"You can talk to me. I'm the commander," she continues.

"It is, what it is," he replies only moving his mouth.

"Naw it's not. I'm going to get onto them about that," she says grabbing his forward from behind his back.

Triple J turns his head and looks at her. Despite the all-black militant uniform she wore, he could see that she was genuinely the sweetest person of them all.

"I'm good Untie. Thank you for being concerned," he replies with a slight smile.

"Yeah, we didn't mean you any harm, Triple J," another officer says standing behind him.

Word must've got to them, he thinks.

After several minutes of standing in the same place the officers finally conclude their search and instructs everyone back to the cells.

"Inmate moving, inmate moving," the officers scream as their walking back in a single file line.

Legal mail, letters, pictures, clothes, hygiene items and commissary were thrown everywhere. When Pop Johnson gets to the cell, he pauses at the door before Triple J sees everything is destroyed. They both look at each other before looking back at the officers and just shake their heads.

Shit Just Got 2 Real

26

_S_everal days after the big shakedown, rumors continue to spread that someone in their crew was snitching. For Triple J it was a struggle to maintain order and at times he wanted to throw in the towel, but his heart wouldn't let him.

It's like every time we take two steps forward, we're pushed back five, Triple J thinks as he's lying in his bunk. _I guess this is my new normal,_ he continues.

In all honesty, he was glad that they were on lockdown. It gave him time to gather his thoughts and focus on his inner self. The shakedown had them going crazy, but his focus was on becoming a better man.

The dorm was on complete lockdown and no one was allowed out of there cell since the shakedown. The only time the cell doors opened was when the officers manually cracked them to pass out food trays. Triple J had no clue to what was happening and couldn't find out with his phone still stashed in the shower but he knew that soon he'll be getting an attorney visit.

As the thought crosses his mind, Officer Price comes over the intercom.

"Triple J! Get dressed you have an attorney visit." Officer Price says calling him by his moniker.

"Let me pray with you before you go son," Pop Johnson says sitting up before climbing off his bed.

He grabs Triple J's hand before bowing his head.

"Dear Heavenly Father, Most Merciful, Most Magnificent, We come to you today with our heads bowed surrendering all to you, all knowing, all mighty God. We understand that this battle is not ours and we pray that you strengthen us with all the tools we need to be victorious in this spiritual war. Father God, we thank you for the all of the blessings that you rain down on us and we pray that you show us how to use these tools. We ask that you deliver us good news today during this attorney visit and strengthen Attorney Torris J with all of the tools and knowledge that he need to do is job at the best capacity. Father God, we thank you, we thank you, we thank you, we thank you in Jesus name Amen."

"Amen," Triple J says.

"Come on Johnson," the officer yells from the 500 entry way, before the cell door begins to open.

Triple J steps out of his cell and the door immediately closes behind him.

"Put your hands behind your back for me Johnson?" The Officer asks him.

He does as he's told before stepping out into the hallway.

"Man the city waiting for you to touchdown," the officer says in a low tone as they're walking to the 700 zone.

Officer McGee was a new Officer Triple J had never seen before. As he stares into his eyes, he sees that he was very young; eighteen or nineteen. Triple J knew that a lot of guys from Atlanta in his age group looked up to the "Triple J Legend," never actually meeting or seeing him personally. Judging his eyes, he sees the excitement and knew he was one of those guys fascinated by the legend.

"I know it Lil brother. I appreciate this lil bid though, on the real. It's given me time to gather my thoughts," Triple J replies.

"I know it, Big Brother let me know if you need me for anything," Officer McGee says.

Triple J knew exactly what he was insinuating, the young officer wanted to get some money. Since transitioning over to The Executive Homies, he had no dealings with the drug game or other illegal activity. Triple J stuck exclusively to helping his homies better themselves by investing into business and entrepreneurship. It was good to know that Officer McGee was down to get some money, Triple J made sure to take note of that.

We'll use him when the time is right.

As he walks up the stairs to the attorney booths in 700, Triple J grips the railing firmly as he's remembering his accident. The last attorney visit he had on the floor; his lawyer informed him of the DA's move for the death penalty. His heart rate rises and butterflies fill his stomach.

We got this shit. Things are going to look bad in the beginning, but will work out in your favor in the end, he reminds himself.

At booth number 3 he sees his lawyer sitting next to a well-dressed white male wearing a royal blue suit.

"Hey Mr. Johnson! This is my good friend Attorney Bryan Steeler. Bryan this is Mr. Johnson," his head attorney Torris J says introducing the two.

"Nice to meet you Mr. Steeler. I've heard so many great things about you," Triple J replies respectfully.

"Nice to meet you as well Triple J. I've heard a lot about you and I'm glad that we've finally met," he replies.

"Now that you two have met let's get down to business. Bryan was looking over your case and it's a lot that he pointed out," Torris J says.

"Yes! So, I don't know if you're familiar with me or not but my main practice is federal and state level criminal appeal cases. I have a team of top tier private investigators with a very high success rate of finding the unfound," Attorney Bryan Steeler begins. "As I was looking over your case, I saw that there was some important information missing. As an attorney, it's my job to comb through and find the small stuff for the greatest impacts. There is a 3-page case summary in your discovery, written by a Detective Emanuel White. Mr. White was involved in one of my appeals cases where he worked illegally undercover," he says before pausing.

Opening the designer leather brief case, Attorney Brian Steeler pulls out a Manila file with several photographs inside. He holds one up to the glass booth and when Triple J sees who's it is his head drops.

Not this nigga, he thinks as he shakes his head.

"Do you know Detective White," Torris J asks. "Do I know him?

Yeah, I know this pig. He was my right hand and now he's sleeping with my wife," Triple J says.

"He's known as E-Man. Did he go by another name?" Attorney Steeler asks.

"JT Wolf!" Triple J answers.

Both attorneys begin to write in their notepads.

Triple J continues to shake his head from left to right. *How did I slip like this?* He asks himself. *I let a pig up on me.*

"I need to ask y'all a legal question. If a police detective is undercover and I ask them directly if they're law enforcement or affiliated with any law enforcement agency, is that a violation of my 5th amendment rights?" He asks.

"This question comes up a lot with street guys. So, in 1990 the higher courts ruled that an undercover government agent at the time is investigating not interrogating so Miranda Laws don't apply. It also wouldn't be a 5th amendment "self-incrimination" violation because the police officer posed as a fellow criminal, leaving out the police dominate atmosphere," Attorney Steeler says before Triple J interrupts him.

"But wouldn't that be entrapment?" Triple J asks.

"No! So, an example of entrapment would be if the undercover officer gives you drugs to sale and then comes back and charge you with drug distribution," Torris J says.

"That's definitely the best example," Attorney Steeler says.

Triple J knew this Detective Emanuel While committed entrapment when he came with the information about Lil CeCe snitching on the family.

I let this fuck nigga up on me, Triple J thinks as he's getting more upset.

"Hey Mr. Johnson look at me. We're working on your defense and I know you live by the street code but you have to tell me everything that you know so we can have a fighting chance," Attorney Steeler says.

Triple J immediately shuts down and refuses to say anything else. He knew exactly what Attorney Bryan Steeler was insinuating for him to do, break the street code and snitch. That was not an option for a man in his position to snitch even on a cop. He couldn't do it.

TJ sees that his client is uncomfortable and concludes the visit.

Shit Just Got 2 Real

or two whole weeks Triple J stays in his cell, even after they're taken off lockdown. A few of his homies stop by to talk but he doesn't say a word to anyone, not even his father. Finding out during the attorney visit that JT Wolf was an undercover detective was so depressing that now he trusts no one.

This nigga had a leadership position. It ain't no telling who he got to flip, Triple J thinks.

The tactical quad didn't find the phones during the big search, so Triple J took full advantage of the opportunity. Using his time with his researching case law, he looked up similar cases to his that were appealed. During the search he found two that really stood out, noting them for his next attorney visit. Testifying on the stand wasn't an option for him but somehow, he had to expose the corrupt undercover detective.

What am I so stressed about? I got all of these lawyers that's already made 3 million off me. It's their job to figure this shit out. Not me! He tries to calm himself.

In the back of his mind though he knew that something had to be done.

I can't kill him, that's gone bring all kinds of unwanted investigations. I can't set him up he gone see it coming. But he is a sucker for a hoe. I gotta find a chick to get up and under him.

As thoughts raced through his mind, he struggles to relax.

A text alert comes though from his attorney's burner phone.

(TJ) *How's things going?*

(Triple J) *It's going. I need to hear some good news.*

(TJ) *We got a major update; I'm coming to see you today. You're going to need to hear this.*

(Triple J) *Hit the horn when you get outside...*

So many different thoughts began to race through his mind as he wonders what major update they have for him. One thing Triple J knows for certain, is that if TJ says it's major, it's MAJOR.

Laying on his bunk he meditates, envisioning himself walking out of the front of the jail. Although he's never physically seen the front of the jail, he could see himself marching out, with every news crew in the nation surrounding him. He knew that when he left, he would need to hire professional security to transport him and all.

Falling into a deeper state of meditation he begins to see greatness manifest in his life. He sees himself becoming very influential with a major social media platform used to inspire so many in all ethnic communities. He sees The Executive Homies reaching record high levels, in different industrial areas creating high paying jobs for everyone in the black community. He sees himself traveling across the world, motivating professional sports teams and coaches. Triple J knew that when he got out everyone would scream his new name, The Executive Homeboy.

Falling asleep with a smile on his face he's awakened by the officer on the intercom.

"Johnson, get dressed you have an attorney visit," the officer in the booth says.

Triple J was already dressed. He checks his phone and sees the text message notifications from his attorney.

He hands his phone to her father and nods his head signaling for him to hold it.

The cell door opens and Triple J exits with his shirt tucked and manila envelope held to his right side. All eyes are locked on him as he exits in the most confident manner ever.

We got this, he says to himself as he marches out.

Triple J moves quickly up the stairs to the attorney booths, almost tripping on the top step. He pauses a quick second clutching the hand rail tight, thanking God that he didn't go tumbling again. On the other side of the glass, he sees both of his attorneys, Torris J and Bryan Steeler sitting next to one another in good spirits.

"Oh man! Mr. Johnson this case has taken a major twist," TJ says getting right to business. "So, Bryan's investigators found some very valuable information we wanted to run past you."

"Okay," Triple J says nervously.

"Yes Mr. Johnson as Torris said before, my investigators are the best. I asked them to find out everything that they could on the murdered victim in your case, Clarence Coleman aka Lil CeCe. Mr. Coleman worked as an confidential informant for the ACP for over eight years. His handler was Detective White and on the day before his murder his sister says she heard him and Detective White arguing over the phone. Clarence used an app on his iPhone that recorded the recent phone conversations with Detective White. Tanisha, Clarence's sister accessed Clarence's iCloud though her phone and recovered several phone recordings in his deleted files. On one of the calls Detective White is heard threatening Clarence, telling him that his days on earth were numbered. The significance of this information is that when my investigators told her that they had a way to catch the real murderer in her brothers' case she happily transferred the audio files. We, now we have them in our possession," Attorney Bryan Steeler says.

Triple J smiles while pressing his hands together in front of his face.

"Okay now tell him the better news," TJ says.

"Oh yeah! It gets better. Since the audio files were deleted, my investigators followed the trail. It led them to the counties Coroner's office where they were able to obtain a copy of the property logs. Mr. Colman's property included one pair of pants and shirt both riddled with bullet holes. A state ID, Casio wrist watch and guest what an iPhone," Attorney Steeler says. "This is so important because the property was released to Detective Emanuel White of the Atlanta City Police before being transported to the crime lab. Remember now the recordings, according to his sister, were found in the deleted files of Mr. Coleman's iCloud. What this means is that someone deleted evidence while it was being transferred to the crime lab."

Triple J knew all of this information to be true because JT Wolf mentioned that his sources inside of the ACP said that this case would never be held against them. The funny thing is JT Wolf is the source. He's the law officer that's been setting him up the whole time.

"So how is this information valuable for us?" Triple J asks.

"Well!" TJ replies before taking a pause. "The last time we spoke you asked about entrapment laws. In this case because Detective White was working undercover, as JT Wolf a high-ranking leader inside of the Apes aNd Wolves crime family, we plan to present the evidence we have to the DA's office as entrapment. Mr. Colman would still be alive if it was not for Detective White orders to kill him. This is entrapment and it's illegal. This is our way of getting these murder charges dropped and RICO case dismissed."

Triple J stares at them both because he knew this is the major break that he's been looking for.

"So, when the DA see's this evidence, what you're saying is that shit is going to be dismissed and all of my guys gone walk?" Triple J asks.

"That's exactly what we are saying," TJ says assuring him.

"Okay let's do it," Triple J replies quickly giving his attorneys the green light to free them all.

"We're going to the court house right now to see the Judge, DA and Assistant DA. Please stay out of trouble in here things are going to be final within the next 30 days," TJ tells him.

"I got you I promise." Triple J says.

As he's walking back to his cell he begins to see himself vividly walking out of the front doors of the Fulton Jail.

Nothing can stop me; he says before walking back into the dormitory.

Shit Just Got 2 Real!

28

*G*rowing up Triple J's father passed on legendary quotes for him to live by. Many of them he received, but some never made sense until his adult years. During this depressing time of incarceration, he gradually recalls his childhood teachings, implementing them into his day-to-day activities.

"Even though your hands belong to the same body, you never let your right hand know what the left is doing," James Jay told his young son.

Those words apply most favorable in today's times because he didn't know who to trust. His understanding of his father's teachings, is that no matter if they're family or not, never let anyone know what you got going on.

Triple J stuck to his silent routine saying nothing about the major updates. He desperately wanted to tell his father but chose to stick to his teachings and remain silent.

Never let your right hand know what your left is doing, he reminds himself again.

As the days go by, he waits patiently to hear an update

from his lawyers. TJ said it would be around 30 days so he counts the days down marking each of them on a sheet of paper. His main thing was to stay out of the way and let everything play out. While he's lying on his bed Triple J hears the Green Team guys enter the dormitory.

"Everybody face the wall," the Sargent Riley of the Green Team screams as he's entering the dormitory.

Everyone stops what they're doing and stand-up walking towards the wall.

Six green team members enter the dormitory and separate forming two groups. Three officers walk to Triple J's cell while the other three stand behind the group of guys facing the wall.

"Johnson! Come cuff up," Sargent Riley says looking at him through the window.

Triple J stands from the bed and complies, immediately assuming that they were there to take him to see Captain James. Placing his hands in front he allows them to apply the handcuffs on him without any problems. Brought out into the hall the officers escort him out, saying not a word. Triple J also keeps his mouth sealed saying nothing as he's escort to the elevators.

"Stand and face the back wall," Sargent Riley says as they step on.

The group of six officers stand behind him and Triple J sense that something is wrong. From the corner of his eye, he sees that Sargent Riley is wearing a body camera and it's recording.

What the hell is going on, Triple J thinks as he stares at the elevator's wall.

They come off the elevators and walk down the same

hallway that first appearance court is held. He still doesn't know where he's going, continuing to walk with his escorts. Around the control booth they go walking down another very long hallway. One of the officers' types in an eight-digit code before the right double door pops open. As they escort him through the double doors Triple J realizes he's in the booking area.

"What are we doing down here?" Triple J asks as they walk pass several holding cells.

"Captain James is going to explain it to you," Sargent Riley says.

Triple J stares in confusion when Captain James stops talking to the older female seated at her desk. She stands and they both begin to walk towards him.

"What's going on?" Triple J asks with a very concerned look in his eyes.

"The GIB backed up the information on a cell phone located inside of the jail and your picture was found inside. It was a picture you sent to your wife," Captain James says.

"So what's going on now?" Triple J asks.

"You're being charged with possession of a prohibited item by inmate," Captain James says.

Triple J shakes his head in confusion because he knew that Captain James told him he would take care of that phone found.

As he's going through the finger printing process again, he remembers Detective White said the same thing and it backfired on him. Captain James hands Triple J an arrest citation as there going through the fingerprinting process. Triple J just shakes his head in disbelief.

Damn man! TJ just told me don't get in no shit, we're all going home, Triple J thinks.

As they're walking off, a man beats on the window of his cell next to them.

"You think you got me? Do you think you got me? You ain't no Ape boy you a sheep," he yells through the crack of the door. "You a sheep boy," He continues.

Triple J looks in the direction of the screams and sees Detective Emanuel White in a jail uniform.

They got him, he thinks. *They finna let us go.*

Triple J smiles at him while he yells in distress.

"You just a sheep boy. You're just a sheep. And you know me and my Wolves gone eat you sheep boy. I'm gone eat you alive sheep boy, I'm gone eat you alive," Detective White continues to yell as they're walking off.

He begins to bark like a wolf in his cell and Triple J continues to smile as he's escorted back to the top floor.

Shit Just Got 2 Real.

Breaking News

"The Fulton Jail has been the home for several members and associates of the ANW crime family for several months now.

Last year we covered a story involving the arrest of its leader, James Johnson, Jr. aka Triple J. Triple J along with 27 other members were recently indicted on felony RICO charges the worst being murder and this morning the DA announced that all charges against the ANW crime family would be dismissed," the news anchor says.

The camera shot changes over to a clip of Detective Emanuel White being escorted by ACP's SWAT members to the back of a police car.

"It's all good! Players fuck up sometimes," Detective White says before the door closes.

"On yesterday, my office presented new found evidence to a grand jury on former ACP major crimes detective. Detective Emanuel White, aka E-Man worked the streets of Atlanta as an undercover government agent. While investigating the Grant Park Apes he was able to infiltrate the organization, merging a group he led the Washington Park Wolves into the ANW crime family. During his assignment Detective White forgot that his first role was to protect and serve the community. Yesterday Detective White was indicted on 17 felony charges the worst being felony murder. Voice recordings of Detective White threatening murdered victim, Clarence "Lil CeCe" Colman, were found during an evidence swab of his iPhone. With this new evidence present Defense Attorney filed a motion to dismiss based on the illegal entrapment role Detective Emanuel White played in this case. A judge ruled in the favor of ANW dismissing all charges against the crime family.

29

Forty-Eight hours after the judge dismissed all charges, 27 of the 28 members listed in the RICO indictment were called over the intercoms to pack it up.

"We out this bitch," one of the homies screams.

"The streets are in trouble now," another one says. "ANW back bitches."

It gets silent for a while after he says that.

"Ain't no more ANW fool. Remember were 'The Executive Homies' now," The Executive Flames says checking him from behind the cell door.

No one knew what was going on, until the news aired the arrest of JT Wolf. Triple J had to tell his close homies that he would be staying back until the new case was resolved. As the guys continue to scream in excitement, Triple J laid on his bunk in amazement.

It's the job of a Boss to make sure his people are straight; he thinks as he lay back on the bunk. *I swear this road has been a long one but I'm thankful I don't have that death penalty shit over my head anymore.*

As he's thinking, the phone conversation with his attorney starts to play back.

"We're going to ask the Judge that you get time serve, but he can give you up to 5 years at his discretion," TJ tells him.

"I can't stay up here no 5 years," Triple J replies.

"No, that 5 will be served in the state under the Department of Corrections supervision," TJ tells him.

Butterflies immediately swarm his belly.

"Damn we done beat all this major shit and I'm still going down the road? For a cell phone?" Triple J asks.

"As I said before Mr. Johnson it's at the Judge's discretion," TJ says.

Five years was a lot of time in prison, but Triple J knew that he could do it.

A boss is going to be a boss, no matter where you put him, he reminds himself.

All of the doors began to open as the officers enter the dorm.

"Y'all some lucky mother-fuckers," Sargent Kennedy a twelve-year veteran with the Sheriff's Office says as he enters. "I just knew y'all niggas was gone get fried. Especially you loud mouth," he continues looking at Flames.

"Fuck you nigga we out this bitch," Flames replies as he walking out of his cell with his property.

"I ain't worried about you being gone for long. I got a hundred dollars you'll be booked back in before the ink dries on your release papers," Sargent Kennedy replies.

"Damn that's fucked up Sarge," Flames replies.

"Naw I'm joking young man. I seen greatness in you when we first met on the 6th floor. Y'all might think I'm lying but I really wanna see y'all guys get out of here and stay out. My biggest wish is for y'all to get out of here and be productive in the community. Some of y'all are parents. Go home and take care of your kids fuck what you and ya baby mama got going on. Take care of them kids. I ain't gone hold y'all up I know y'all ready to go I just wanna say this before y'all leave. Please stay out of trouble. I don't wanna see y'all back in here," Sargent Kennedy says with genuine love in his voice.

His warm words could be felt throughout the entire dorm. No one wanted to be locked up but the mere reality for them was that at least one of them would. It's a struggle for Triple J watching his guys leave and his father knew that.

"Ecclesiastics 3:3 says it's a time for everything son. Your time is coming and I promise you that every single one of us is going to be outside that gate waiting to pick you up," his father says.

Triple J truly believed that but deep down it still caused him pain.

I'm gone bounce back. And when I do it's going to be way harder than I did before I left.

As their filing out to leave all of his homies stop by his cell to say goodbye.

"You gone be good Big Homie we all waiting for you," one of them says.

As they're giving there farewells many of them drop off there excess commissary items with him. Leaving so much behind, Triple J had at least ten of everything making his cell look like a convince store when it was all said and done.

After all of his homies were gone the dormitory was left in silence. Triple J gave away his phone and the three phones left behind, to the guys in there with him. Since the new charges he didn't want anything else that could cost him more time of his life.

Laying on the bunk he tries his best to rest before the anxiety takes over. After several hours of mind wondering, he's finally able to go to sleep. Around 3am his cell door cracks open and closes right back. Triple J swears he's dreaming when he sees his jail house girlfriend in front of him.

Lieutenant Rodgers stands in front of him wearing a gray Sheriff's Department jogging suit.

"Why you acting like you see a ghost or something?" She asks. "You know got damn well I been waiting to get some of that good dick," she continues.

Triple J sits up on the bunk rubbing his eyes to make sure he's not tripping.

"Wake up nigga! We ain't got that much time," she says in a low aggressive tone.

Triple J stands from the bunk slowly and she pushes him back down. She falls to her knees in a soft and fluid motion sending a tingle through his body.

"I got this. Just relax Daddy," she says seductively.

Lt. Rodgers pulls over her hoodie, revealing her beautiful round breast. Triple J reaches to caress them but she pushes him back on the bunk.

"I said relax," she says taking the dominant role.

Reaching into his pants, she pulls out his half limp penis. Kissing the tip with her luscious lips.

"Damn I needed this," Triple J says as he's placing his hand on her head.

She slides her warm mouth down his manhood, while squeezing at the bottom with her hand.

"Hiss" Triple J sounds off while exhaling from the oral suction.

She continues to slurps up and down his rod, causing his eyes to roll into the back of his head. Lt. Rodgers knew exactly what she was doing as she gobbled on his rod like a professional porn star.

"This that shit I like," she says to him while kissing more on his dick.

Standing up and turning around she shuffles her round and brown ass from left to right. While pulling down her pants she pops her ass up and down twerking in front of him.

"You like that?" She asks while looking back at him with her knees bent.

Between her legs she reaches and grabs his Johnson. Guiding his dick inside of her wet ass pussy, she jerks as the thick girth spreads her insides.

"Whew! It feel like you've gotten bigger," she says as she exhales.

Using her vagina muscles, she squeezes his penis as she bounces up and down.

"Yes Lawd," Triple J says smacking his hands on her ass checks.

He quickly catches himself, remember that they were sneaking and other people could possibly hear them.

Lt. Rodgers is a control freak that likes to be in charge but Triple J was stressed out. Grabbing her around the waist he spins her around with his dick still inside and push her head into the mat.

He slams his dick deep inside of her as she tries to run.

"You ain't going nowhere bitch," Triple J says while growling his teeth.

Smashing her little tight pussy from the back Lt Rogers screams inside of his makeshift pillow.

"Yeah bitch, who in charge now? I said who in charge now bitch?" Triple J asks her.

"I'm in ch-arge!" She yells at him in between pumps. "I'm in fu-ucking ch-arge."

Triple J laughs before taking things to another gear. Grabbing both of her arms he puts them behind her back. While pulling her to him he throws dick into her chest while clapping her ass cheeks against his lap

"Oh yeah! You in charge right?" Triple J asks while continuing to wear her out.

"Um-mmm," she squirms while shaking her head from side to side. "Ooh I love dis d-ick. I lo-ve dis dick," she screams at him.

Triple J says nothing he continues to pound her none stop finding that sweet spot in the pockets of her guts.

"I'm about to cum," she yells. "I'm about to cum."

Triple J slaps her on the ass, while still pounding her violently.

"Oh my Gawd, oh my Gawd daddy. You're in charge. You're charge." She continues to yell.

Triple J continues to kill her guts wearing her out until he reaches his climax. His body locks up and he's ready to explode inside of her.

"Boom, boom, boom," the officer knocks on his window with the flash light.

"Wake up Johnson you got court this morning," he says.

Triple J looks around the room and sees there is no one in there but him.

Ain't no way bra.

Shit Just Got 2 Real!

ourt days are the worst days, in the Fulton Jail, especially for Triple J since everybody knows him. Those that didn't, wanted to know him so it was a gift and a curse for the ex-crime boss.

Awakened at 4am he quickly takes a shower, cleaning himself from the wet dream debris in his pants.

"Damn that shit felt real," he says aloud thinking about his early morning extravaganza with Lt. Rodgers.

Dressed and ready to go, he sits at the dayroom table with a belly full of nervousness.

These folks trying to send a nigga to prison God and this ain't right. I know I haven't been the best person in the world but you know my heart I try. I know that trying isn't an excuse for disobedience but please don't let these folks send me to prison. I've changed and I'm willing to work for you in the streets. I know you have the power to switch this thing around so today I'm trusting you to do the right thing for heaven's sake,

Amen.

As soon as he finishes his prayer the officer calls for him into the hall.

"Johnson let's go," she says.

Triple J stands and walks out the door into the 700 zone. Four out of the eight guys going to court today were in there already waiting. Only two of them have legal envelopes in their hands, Triple J and another guy, showing that they were prepared.

"You're Triple J right," one of the older guys ask him.

"Unfortunately, I am," Triple J answers.

"That's a fortunate thing young man. Don't you know how many people speak highly of you?" He asks.

"Yeah, I know. I need them to tell the judge today," Triple J replies.

The old man understood what he was saying. No matter how good a person talk about you it's no good in this racial justice system. A black man in America was exactly that, a black man in America. It doesn't matter how much money you have you're still a black man in America.

"You're gonna be alright young man just keep your faith," he tells Triple J trying to encourage him.

"Will do!" Triple J replies with a head nod.

The doors to 900 opens and two male officers walk in. Behind them are three inmates two handcuffed together with the other cuffed to the front.

"Where are y'alls chain train," One of the officers asks the female officer.

"On Sarge desk," she replies looking towards the office.

One of the officers go in and grabs it before placing handcuffs on one hand of each individual going to court.

They quickly go down the elevator to the holding cells near the rear sally port.

"Y'all have a good day at court. If you don't know what to do always remember numbers are much better than letters," the officer says before leaving.

Triple J shakes his head in agreement knowing that they were just seeking letters in his case, The Death Penalty. Although he didn't want to do any more time he was thankful that now all they could give him was five years.

Since Triple J was a high-profile inmate the transport deputies separated him from the rest of the group. Placed in waist chains and shackles, Triple J's is escorted outside by two veteran deputy Sargent's.

"Watch your head," the deputy Sargent says as he's placing Triple J in the back of his Charger police car.

Triple J climbs in and falls down on the hard plastic back seat.

"You good?" The Deputy asks before closing the door.

"Yeah but can I get some air?" Triple J asks.

"We're about to get rolling in a minute. I'll let down your window when we start riding," the Sargent answers him.

Triple J knew that the police was some bull shit, but couldn't let this one ride.

"How can y'all lock a motherfucker up for leaving a dog in a hot car? But then you tell me you gone let the window down when we start riding."

"The dog not lock up you is nigga. Now shut the fuck up, I'll be back," the officer says before slamming the door on Triple J's arm.

Angry and vengeful he had to catch himself from going overboard. Triple J knows he's a powerful man that can get the deputies killed for nothing, but right now he was power-less. He's a man with no control, headed to a courtroom for another man to make judgement over his life. A tear rolls down his eye as he thinks about his life.

"I know this is not the way my life was written. This shit gotta be a dream," he says to himself before closing his eyes.

Sleeping the entire ride, Triple J wakes up as they are pulling into the courthouse basement. He gets out of the car and doesn't say a word until he gets upstairs and sees his attorneys.

"How you doing Mr. Johnson," his attorney asks excited and full of energy.

"I'm just ready to go home," Triple J replies.

"I am as well I know you're ready to get back to your family. I got you some good news though," TJ says.

"What's that?"

"The State offered us a plea of 3 years to be served on first offenders' probation so that you don't have a record when this is all over," TJ says.

"3 years' probation," he repeats. "Tell them I'll do it if I can go home today," he continues.

"That's what we're going for," TJ replies before he walks off.

Two of the court house deputies escort Triple J into a jam-packed courtroom. Several media stations were filming his every move. The Assistant DA passed his attorney a sheet of paper with all of the information on it pertaining to the plea deal and his attorney signed before Triple J signed.

"Let me know when y'all are ready," The Judge says in his deep baritone voice.

"Yes sir, Your Honor," The ADA replies. "We'll be ready shortly."

"I told you I was going to get you out," Torris J says to his client while smiling from ear to ear.

Two sheriff's deputy escorts Triple J and his attorney to the podium for court to begin.

"We're ready, Your Honor," The Assistant DA says.

"Okay you all can begin," the Judge says.

"Your Honor we bring before you today, The State vs. James Johnson Jr. possession of a prohibited item by inmate. A guilty plea is being entered and the states offer is 3 years to be served on first offenders' probation," The ADA says.

"What's Mr. Johnson initial reason for being in custody?" The judge asks.

"Mr. Johnson also known as Triple J in his community was initially arrested on murder charges that later lead to a RICO indictment. That case was recently dismissed," the ADA replies.

"Do you know why that case was dismissed?" The Judge asks.

"Yes! Your Honor. Mr. Johnson's case was dismissed after evidence was found of a state officer, working undercover, abused his powers to entrap the defendants," the ADA answers.

"But nothing that showed he was innocent of the crime?" The judge asks.

Neither Triple J nor his attorney understands why the judge was so concerned about the dismissed case. It had nothing to do with this one.

"Does the defense have anything that they would like to say?" The judge asks.

"Yes! Your Honor. My client is being charged with a cell phone that was not found in his possession or the dormitory in which he was housed. After GIB investigators searched through the phone it's said that a photo of my client was found in the recovered deleted files. We would have disputed these charges but my client felt that serving 3 years on first offenders' probation would be a whole lot easier than sitting another day incarcerated," Torris J says.

The judge never looks at Triple J during the entire hearing and he realizes that.

"I've listened to both sides and I agree that three years on first offenders' probation would be a fair plea for a jail house cell phone. Hell, I wish the one that gave him the phone was here in front of me today. I would have agreed to this plea deal if it was an average Joe but it's not. We're talking about Mr. Triple J the man who says he runs the A. I'm convinced that Mr. Triple J used his money and power to force an innocent young woman to bring him that phone. I know people like Triple J see themselves above the law and for that reason I'm sentencing you to 5 years without the possibility of parole. No jail credit will be given I want you to serve the entire 5 under the supervision of the Department of Corrections," the judge says staring at Triple J with an evil look in his eyes before slamming the gavel.

Both Triple J and his attorney look at each other in shock.

Shit Just Got 2 Real.

AUTHORS LETTER

In the American society, most of us have had some type of run in with the law, from traffic stops to major felonies. Standing in the court room waiting to receive judgement is one of the hardest things one can go through.

In this book series, I wanted to give real examples of how the powerful become powerless. I wanted to show the struggles one goes through to find peace under the darkness of incarceration. I hope you feel the emotional feeling I put into this book and understand that despite what you see on social media it's really hard doing time.

I wanna thank all of my readers and supporters for sharing this experience with me a second time. It's been a roller coaster ride preparing this book but we've made it.

I want to thank my family and friends especially my Auntie Gaati Werema for helping me in so many ways with this work. She's the Best! I wanna thank my legal and financial aids. My counselors for keeping me inspired when I wanted to give up. And I wanna thank myself. It's been hard but I did it and I hope you enjoy

Thank You,
The Executive Homeboy

DID YOU ENJOY THIS BOOK!

Publishers/Authors Contact:

DID YOU ENJOY THIS BOOK!

The Executive Homeboy
www.theexecutivehomeboy.com
4045009979